Wendy Gill was born in Barnsley, South Yorkshire, in 1944, the youngest daughter of John and Connie Moxon. She attended Ardsley Oaks Junior and Infant School, then Oaks Secondary Modern, leaving at the age of fifteen.

She met Kevin and they married in 1964. They have two children – a son, Spencer, and daughter, Deborah.

She retired at the age of sixty-one and took up writing as a pastime.

The Fat Man and His Toad

WENDY GILL

The Fat Man and His Toad

Vanguard Press

VANGUARD PAPERBACK

© Copyright 2015
Wendy Gill

A CIP catalogue record for this title is
available from the British Library.

ISBN 978 178465 031 5

Vanguard Press is an imprint of
Pegasus Elliot Mackenzie Publishers Ltd.
www.pegasuspublishers.com

First Published in 2015

Vanguard Press
Sheraton House Castle Park
Cambridge England

Printed & Bound in Great Britain

Acknowledgements

For his patience and understanding to my husband, Kevin,
and to my sisters, Valerie Owen and Carol Wood,
for their enthusiasm and encouragement.

CHAPTER 1

The belt came down, landing in the middle of her back.

"All right, you win," she told him.

Gary Farnsworth stood over his daughter breathing heavily.

"About time too," he gasped. "Tomorrow, outside at nine o'clock and woe-betide you if you don't appear." He threw the belt down and walked out pushing aside the young man who had been watching the proceedings with a malicious smirk on his face.

"I knew you'd cave in, should've said yes in the first place and saved yourself the beating. You're a fool, all that money and the big house. The likes of you should be grabbing at the chance," he sneered.

"The likes of me have seen enough of men to last me a lifetime. You're animals, all of you, so I might as well marry this stupid lord. At least I won't have to set eyes on either of you two again," she spat back.

"Oh you'll be seeing plenty of us once you're married to Lord Planter, there's plenty of money to go round. After all, I'm sure he'll see his father-in-law and brother-in-law all right."

"Not if I can help it, you'll get nothing from his estate. I'll try and prevent it even if I end up six feet under by doing so."

A laugh escaped the young man and he followed his father outside.

Harriett had to take hold of the old bedstead to pull herself up. Blood began to soak through the material of the old cotton dress that had once belonged to her mother. She was nineteen years old and had lived in this rundown shack in the middle of the moors all her life. Even though isolated they had been happy and carefree years. Her mother had been alive then. She had protected her from Gary Farnsworth and her brother; they had treated her with respect, albeit at arm's length. They didn't have much to do with each other.

Her mother, Lady Freda West, had also lived a pretty sheltered life growing up with her parents some fifteen miles away on a moderate estate called Crag Farm. It had provided a wealthy living for them. They also had a house in the city and when Lady Freda was eighteen years old they took her to her first season. She was rigged out with pretty, modern and expensive gowns and was one of the most courted young ladies that season.

Unbeknown to her parents Lady Freda had formed an attachment to one of the young bucks and their passion for each other was at times over enthusiastic and before returning home at the end of the season, Lady Freda knew she was with child.

Unexpectedly Lady Freda's mother had been taken ill and within a few days of returning home she had passed away.

Her father was devastated and took to gambling and drinking and within a month, Lady Freda's idyllic life was turned upside down.

He father was unapproachable and she was almost three months pregnant. She had written to her handsome young man, no mention of the baby, and he had replied saying he was riding down to Crag Farm the following Monday.

On the Sunday morning Lady Freda decided to walk across the moors to church. Halfway there she bumped into Gary Farnsworth, a no good layabout from the neighbouring village. He tore her clothes, raped her, left her on the moors and went on his way.

Lady Freda made her way home and stumbled into the library and told her father of the rape. Before her mother's death, Freda had been able to talk to her father about anything but in the end he told her she would have to marry the man who had raped her to make an honest woman of her. She tried to tell her father that a young man she had met in Drunbury was calling to see her the next day but he refused to let her see him and locked her in her bedroom.

When her young man arrived he was told by her father he could not see her and that she had met someone else and didn't want to have any more to do with him.

Locked in her bedroom Lady Freda stood sobbing at the window watching him ride away.

Her father made her marry Gary Farnsworth in a private service at Crag Farm. When she was walking out of the library she turned, and looked at him with such pleading in her sad scared eyes that her father turned away in shame. No sooner had the door closed behind her than she heard a gunshot and ran back into the library to find her father slumped over his desk with blood running over the desk top. The pistol was still in his hand.

If Gary Farnsworth thought he was going to inherit Crag Farm he got a rude awakening. When the will was read Harriett learnt that her father had died a pauper and the farm had to be sold to pay off debts.

The rundown shack that Gary Farnsworth lived in had then become Lady Freya's home. Located in the middle of the deserted moor it suited Lady Freda perfectly, she could never show her face in polite society again.

Harriett was born six months later, a beautiful baby girl with strawberry blonde hair and peaches and cream complexion.

Three months after Harriett was born Gary raped Freda again and this time Freda told Gary that if he ever touched her again she'd stab him in his sleep. He knew she'd keep her word but it was too late, Freda found herself with child again and Harriett ended up with a younger brother whom they named Ronald.

Freda did her best to love Ronald but as he got older he turned out to be more and more like his father. Where they went and what they did Freda didn't want to know.

Surviving on food they had grown and what little Gary provided. There was never any money for new clothes so the clothes they wore were what Freda had brought with her. By the time Harriett was sixteen the shared wardrobe was very sparse indeed.

On Harriett's seventeenth birthday Gary told Freda that it was about time they looked for a husband for her because he'd kept her long enough.

Freda told Gary for the first time that Harriett wasn't his daughter and that she'd been pregnant when he raped her. From that day forth Gary made Freda's life a misery. Freda finally lost the will to live and she passed away twelve months later.

Harriett continued to live with Gary Farnsworth and her brother. They kept her as an unpaid slave. She had nowhere else to go. She had no option but to stay and no matter how badly she was treated she was determined not to let them drag her down like they had her mother.

Sleep didn't come easily for Harriett that night. She lay in bed with a throbbing back and thoughts of what was in store for her. These thoughts terrified her but she was determined to get away from there no matter what the cost.

Harriett watched as Gary Farnsworth (she refused to call him father) and her brother had an uncustomary wash and put on clean clothes. She made no such effort. Her self-hygiene was usually faultless but today the only thing she changed was her dress as the other one was stained at the back with dried blood. Her mother had taught her to wash everyday but today, she decided to rebel and left herself unwashed.

Gary Farnsworth turned and looked at her. She stood with back straight, her head held high and her hands folded in front of her. "You'd better not let me down, Harry," Gary said. "I'll not be thwarted on this. You'll marry this man or you may disappear and not been seen again. It's a big moor and there are isolated places where a body will never be found." He held her gaze.

"Don't worry I'll go through with it. I might as well be one man's slave as two. I can't wait to get the stink of this place off me. The sooner I leave the better," she replied.

Five miles to the north Lord Nicholas Planter was heading for their shack accompanied by a vicar and his best friend, Lord Anthony Tandleson, who was leading a spare horse.

"Nicky, this is madness. For goodness sake, let's turn back. A promise extracted in a drunken stupor, my God man what are you about?" his friend demanded.

"Drunk or not, it was a promise I made and I intend to keep it. I have found that on the whole females are all the same, offering you everything but in actual fact giving you nothing. I am twenty-nine years old and have known my fair share of women and none have come up to my expectations. I have to marry sometime so why not to this woman? At least I know where I stand with her. If she's expecting me to be a walkover she has another thing coming," was the reply.

As the three men approached the shack they saw two men standing outside. One of the men Lord Planter recognised from the tavern, the younger version standing next to him, he did not know. There was no female to be seen.

Reining in their horses the three travellers jumped down and they all stood looking at each other.

Gary Farnsworth turned his head and shouted, "Harry, out here, now."

A few seconds elapsed and there was no sign of Harriett.

"I'll just go and get her, my lord, she's a bit shy," Gary said.

But before he could move the door opened and out came a young woman with head held high. Ignoring her persecutors she walked over to the three strangers and stood looking from one to the other. For a fleeting moment Lord Planter thought he'd seen the young woman somewhere before but realised it must have been a trick of the light.

The vicar stepped forward and reading her name off the special marriage licence he said, "Miss Harriett Farnsworth?"

"That's me," she affirmed in a clear strong voice.

The marriage ceremony was short and to the point and straight after, Lord Planter mounted his horse giving the reins of the spare horse to Harriett. She took hold of them and waited to be assisted up onto the back of the horse.

Harriett, never having ridden on horseback before in her life did not want to show herself up. She saw that the saddle was a side-saddle and remembered her mother telling her how she had learned to ride a horse from being very young and she had become a very competent horsewoman. It was the fashion for young ladies to ride side-saddle.

Lord Tandleson came to Harriett's aid by cupping his hands together so she could use them as a stirrup and he hoisted her up. He heard her give a gasp and he glanced up to see her eyes closed and her lips pressed tightly together.

"Are you all right?" he asked.

"Fine," she answered but Lord Tandleson noted how quiet she was and it seemed to be an effort for her to reply.

After checking that the young woman was safely seated on the horse Lord Tandleson nodded to his friend and the wedding party set off back across the moor.

Harriett clung onto the pummel for dear life, her back screamed out with pain at the jolting of the horse. To make things worse the sun was beating down and she had no hat on. Nor had she had anything to eat that morning. She thought the journey would never end.

Her head was getting lower and lower, her back and legs aching, but she did not fall off. She had her eyes closed now and the horse just followed the others until they came to an abrupt halt. Harriett felt herself falling sideways and sliding off the horse.

CHAPTER 2

Lord Planter had dismounted and handed his horse to the waiting stable boy. As he was passing Harriett's horse she was sliding off. He caught her in his arms, carried her inside, up the broad staircase, kicked a bedroom door open and dumped her unceremoniously on top of the bed. Without a further glance he turned and walked out closing the door behind him.

Two hours later Harriett woke to find herself still fully clothed on top of an enormous bed in an enormous bedroom. The room was nearly as big as the entire shack she had just left. Her head ached. In fact her whole body ached. She sat up gingerly and slowly removed her gown, which was stuck to her back with dried blood; it had started to bleed again. Lifting the covers she crawled into bed feeling the soft cool sheets on her naked bleeding back and slid back into oblivion.

For the next two days she came in and out of consciousness. She found food and water left on a tray at the side of the bed. She ate and drank then crawled back under the covers.

Having not seen his wife since he dumped her on the bed, Lord Planter pulled the bell at the side of the fireplace.

Wrenshaw, his butler, entered the room and he was instructed to have his wife brought down into the library straight away.

Wrenshaw headed for the kitchen and instructed the chambermaid, Sally, to go up into the new Lady Planter's bedroom and tell her that Lord Planter wanted to see her in the library.

Word got around the servants of the circumstances that surrounded the marriage of his lordship. Most of them, being his old retainers, felt resentment towards the new Lady Planter.

Sally nervously knocked on the bedroom door but got no response. She slowly opened the door and went in. She saw a red face with strawberry blonde hair lying against a white pillowcase fast asleep. Taking hold of her shoulder, Sally shook her and two green eyes opened and looked blankly at the young girl with a white-mop cap covering her mouse-brown hair standing over her.

"Begging your pardon, my lady, but you are to join his lordship in the library immediately. I have been sent to fetch you."

It took Harriett a few seconds to come round, still feeling sick, sore and stiff. She remembered her fate but her old reserve kicked in and she told the maid to wait outside and she would join her shortly. Her head swam as she sat up. She saw the tray of food and drink at her bedside. Whilst she pulled on her old dress she ate the bread and drank the cold tea. She had eaten and drunk worse in her short lifetime.

A few minutes later she joined the young girl waiting outside her bedroom door and followed her silently down the broad staircase, across a wide black and white tiled hall and through the door that Sally held open for her. Still feeling light-headed, Harriett took a couple of steps into the room and felt her knees begin to buckle so she stood still, closed her eyes and took a few deep breaths.

"Sit down," Lord Planter ordered from behind a big oak desk. He did not look up when he heard the door open and close.

"I'll stay where I am, no doubt what you have to say to me won't take long," came the unexpected reply.

This remark stopped Lord Planter's pen from moving across the paper and, looking across the room, he saw his newly acquired wife standing by the door dressed in the same dress she had arrived in. "You'll find my mother's clothes in the wardrobes in the room you occupy. Make use of any of the things in that room but nothing from anywhere else in the house. Is that understood?"

"Thank you, that's most generous of you, I only hope your mother won't mind," she replied.

"The devil she won't, she's been dead these past eight years. The moths might have taken a liking to them though, so you had better go through them and make sure there are no holes where no holes should be."

"I've shared with worse things than moths, I'm sure we'll get on splendidly," she said in an even voice.

Lord Planter, unused to insolence was beginning to get rattled. He gave her a steady look and their eyes met across the room, neither of them breaking eye contact until the door swung open hitting Harriett in the middle of the back sending shock waves through her body. Her legs buckled and she dropped to her knees trying not to breathe in too deeply until the pain eased.

Wrenshaw saw the lady on her hands and knees as he entered the room and held out a hand to help her stand, which she took gratefully but kept her head down as she struggled to regain her composure.

"Are you afflicted by some sort of falling down sickness?" Lord Planter asked her.

"Only since I made your acquaintance, my lord," she told him.

"What did you want, Wrenshaw?" his lordship asked his butler.

"I beg your pardon, my lord. Mrs Raynor wanted to know what time you wanted dinner."

"Tell her the usual time but I will be leaving for the city tomorrow morning, early. Ask Evans to pack and inform the stable to be ready for six o'clock. I want an early start."

"Very good, my lord. Will Lady Planter be travelling with you?"

"No, Wrenshaw, she will not."

"Very good, my lord." Wrenshaw left the room.

"As you just heard I leave for the city tomorrow. I don't know how long I will be away. I have arranged with my secretary to give you an allowance each month and not a penny more. If you want new clothes you will have to pay for them out of the allowance. Don't be thinking you're going to have a free hand at spending my money because you are not."

Lord Planter looked across at her, waiting for her reply.

"Am I to pay the cook for my meals out of the allowance also?" she asked.

"Damn it, woman, *no*! Did your mother not teach you any manners?" he asked.

"My mother taught me that respect has to be earned. So far you have not come up to my standards." She held his gaze.

"Very well, if this is how it's going to be let battle commence. You are dismissed."

"Thank goodness for that, my lord. For a moment there I thought I was in for a lecture." She took hold of her skirt, lifted if slightly, curtsied, then turned and left the speechless lord staring at the closed door.

Harriett made her way back to her bedroom and found fresh water and some bread and cold meat on the bedside table. She sat on the bed and ate hungrily. She undressed and climbed back into bed and once more into oblivion.

The next morning Lord Planter gave a final glance round half hoping to see his wife standing in the doorway to see him off. There was no sign of her. He mounted his horse and set off at a steady gallop down the winding drive. Still lazing in bed, he thought. Well when he returned things would be different. He had no idea how these thoughts would come back and haunt him.

Waking that same morning feeling much better, Harriet found more bread and butter but this time the water was replaced with a glass of creamy milk. The only time Harriett had been treated to breakfast in bed was on her birthdays when her mother would bring her a boiled egg with thin slices of bread and butter. She thought it a treat fit for a king.

The door opened and Sally walked in. "We have been instructed by Lord Planter to bring all your meals up here and to make sure you don't go wandering about the house until he returns."

"Thank you, I will stick to my room, but am I allowed outside? Surely I am not to be kept a prisoner?"

"No, my lady, you may wander around outside as much as you please." Making a quick curtsey, Sally turned and fled.

If Lord Planter thought he was punishing Harriett by restricting her to this room he was sadly mistaken. The big double bed was the centrepiece but the room also boasted two huge wardrobes and a comfortable looking armchair at the side of a large open fireplace. A small writing desk flanked one wall, but more than anything about the room Harriett let her eyes linger on the extensive bookshelves that ran from floor to ceiling: luxury! On the opposite side a double set of bow windows with heavy brocade curtains opened onto an immaculately kept vista with a wide-sweeping drive leading, Harriett presumed, down to the main entrance.

She could not remember entering the grounds or even going to bed.

Lord Planter had said that this was to be her room and everything in it. Harriett went over to the wardrobes and found them full of beautiful expensive gowns. Looking at them she thought they looked about her size. She took out a plain, grey, woollen, semi-fitted dress and tried it on. It fitted her body perfectly but the length was far too long. Lady Planter must have been a very tall woman.

Still feeling a little shaky, she didn't feel very much like going out. Harriett took the dress and laid it across the armchair whilst she went in search of needle and thread. She found what she was looking for in a wooden sewing box at the side of the writing desk and, making herself comfortable in the huge leather armchair, she set about shortening the garment.

Harriett dozed in the chair and when she woke up the sun had gone down and the moon was shining into the bedroom through the open curtains. Laying the dress aside she closed the curtains, got undressed and curled up in her big four-poster bed.

CHAPTER 3

Waking early, Harriett ate the food that had been, once again, left at the side of her bed. Then she went over to the washstand and had a strip wash before getting dressed. She was feeling much better. Her back still pained her on occasions but her face was less red. This had been caused by being out in the blazing sun on the journey to The Manor. Harriett brushed her hair and looked at her reflection in the long mirror. She was really pleased with her new grey woollen dress; it fitted her perfectly now it was the right length. She had found some soft, leather, ankle boots at the bottom of one of the wardrobes. She had expected them to be far too big for her but to her surprise they fitted snugly and they were the most comfortable boots that had ever graced her feet.

There was a knock on the door and Sally walked in. "I am to be your personal maid."

"Thank you, Sally, but I don't need a personal maid. As you can see I am quite capable of dressing myself," Harriett told her.

"His lordship's instruction," Sally insisted.

"Well, Sally, as you can see I am up and dressed but I would appreciate it if you could have a packed lunch and a bottle of water made up for me. I am going out and won't be back until tea-time." Harriett smiled at her.

"Very good, my lady." Sally gave a small curtsey and left the room.

When the door closed Harriett sat on the edge of the bed. The enormity of her change in circumstances was just beginning to hit her. She didn't think she would ever get used to being called 'my lady' and she certainly didn't want a maid. Her mother had brought her up to be independent and proud despite her family background. She could live without money; she had all she needed in this room: beautiful clothes, soft shoes, huge bed with clean cool sheets and a whole wall full of books.

Harriett turned around and surveyed the wall behind her. She hadn't had time to choose one yet but she savoured the moment when she would select one of the books and be able to read to her heart's content.

Sally came back into the bedroom and held out a small canvas bag. "Thank you, Sally," was all she could think of to say.

Harriett left the house, closing the big heavy oak doors behind her. Looking right then left she decided to go right. She was on an adventure of discovery. With her little canvas bag she set off at a leisurely pace heading nowhere in particular. She walked across the lawn heading for the wood, having all day with nothing to do. There hadn't been many days like this since her mother had passed away.

Harriett couldn't believe her luck. Lord Planter had gone off somewhere and left her alone. If he thought she would think he was snubbing her, he was sadly mistaken. She had roamed the moors from childhood, knowing the surrounding area like the back of her hand. She knew how to check for landmarks if she was somewhere she hadn't been before, to guide her back the way she had come.

Harriett decided to go to Welldeck village and thought going through the wood might cut off a big corner if she could only find her way. The wood was not very dense and she came out of it to find herself in a clearing with dilapidated cottages scattered around. There were women with children feeding hens or hanging washing on a line but no sign of any men. Harriett approached one of the women and, smiling, said, "Hello, I'm sorry to disturb you. I'm trying to find my way to Welldeck. Could you point me in the right direction?"

"If you go back the way you came then bear to the right it takes you to The Manor wall. You will see a mound up against the wall. You have to climb up and over the wall to get onto the Welldeck road or you could go back to the main gate and follow the footpath but it takes a lot longer. It's about three miles as the crow flies when you hop over the wall," she was told.

"Do you all work for Lord Planter?" Harriett asked.

"We do, if you can call it work. He's let the home farm go since his father died. I don't think he's been down to check on things for the past two years. Look at the state of the cottages. When his father was alive he looked after his farmhands, now it's all we can do to make a living for ourselves let alone provide for the estate," she was told.

"The servants up at The Manor seem to be well cared for," Harriett said.

"That they are, they turn their noses up at us farm workers. They live in a warm dry house while we live in squalor and there's poor little Mark Jones, coughing fit to drop and hardly any roof over his head. I don't think he'll survive another winter here but there's nowhere else for us to go."

"Is there nobody who can repair the roofs and replace the broken windows?" she asked.

"The men are out in the fields tending to the crops as best they can, and anyway they have no tools to do the repairs with. There are some building materials in the old barn over there if only we could get someone to do the work. Do you mind if I ask who you are?" enquired the woman.

"I am Lady Planter, and I'm sorry to find you all in this squalor, I'll see what I can do," Harriett told her, then walked away.

She didn't go back to The Manor gates. She followed the instructions back through the wood and found the well-established grass-covered mound of earth piled up against the retaining wall. She scrambled up it, hoisting herself onto the top then swinging her legs over, she hung by her hands before letting herself drop neatly onto the grass on the other side. The footpath was well trodden and Harriett set off at a brisk pace heading for Welldeck. She glanced around a couple of times getting her bearings and was soon in sight of the small bustling village she knew so well.

Harriett passed pie sellers and food stalls set out on the village square and made her way towards the other end of the village. She passed a milliner's shop and saw a notice in the window saying SEAMSTRESS WANTED, barely giving it a glace as she walked on. Stopping outside a shop with wooden stools and chairs outside, she looked in the window but could see no sign of life so she carried on round to the back of the shop.

In the backyard a young man was busy sawing wood and she ran up to him and tapped him on the shoulder. The young man jumped and spun round and seeing his lifelong friend he grinned from ear to ear and said, "Harry, you scared the living daylights out of me. What are you doing here? If Mr Bradley catches you he'll more than likely dismiss me. Where have you been these past couple of weeks?"

"The Fat Man has kept me busy. I've got married but more importantly, I've got you a new job, Jimmy, and I think it comes with a cottage. Come on, get your things and let's go." Harriett grinned.

"Are you out of your mind? Do you expect me to just up and leave, and what do you mean you've got married?" demanded her friend.

"Yes, Jimmy, I do want you to up and leave and I'll tell you all about being married when we're on our way. I have thought about it very carefully on the way here and I think it's the best thing to do," she replied.

"Is this another one of your mad schemes, Harry? You tumble into one scrape after another and expect me to follow. Now you want me to up and leave my job as though it was an everyday event. Do you know how long it took me to get this job?" he asked.

"Of course I do and I also know that Mr Bradley treats you worse than his dog. He hardly pays you anything and lets you sleep in his rat-infested cellar and he thinks he's doing you a favour. Well it's the other way round. You're a brilliant carpenter, Jimmy, and I've found you the perfect job. Go get your tools; I'll help you carry them. Let's get going, there's a lot to be done before winter. You'll love it, you'll see."

"Who am I going to be working for then, tell me that?"

"Lord Planter."

"Who's he?" he asked.

"My husband," Harriett told him.

"Your husband, Lord Planter is your husband?" asked the astonished Jimmy.

"Yes."

"Does he know about this?"

"Well, not exactly."

"How much does this job pay?"

"Nothing, it pays nothing."

"So in a nutshell you want me to pack in my job to come with you to a job that pays nothing, for a man that knows nothing about it and you *think* there's a cottage that goes with it. Is that correct?"

"Yes, come on, let's go."

"Harry, you do know I'm a cripple, don't you?"

"Of course I do, but I don't hold that against you," she told him. "Anyway you've only got one leg a couple of inches shorter than the other and you walk with a limp. That's not a cripple; you don't need crutches or anything. Stop using it as an excuse and go get your things," she insisted.

"Harry, this is madness, I can't just up and leave."

"Why not, you hate both the job and Mr Bradley? Here's a chance to come and live in the country and have your own little cottage, you'll love it. Come on Jimmy for once in your life take a risk."

For a few seconds Jimmy stood looking at her dumbfounded. Harriett was right, he did hate working here and she was also right about having nothing to lose. The picture she'd painted of him living in the country in a little cottage of his own was too much to resist. Turning he went inside and down into the cellar. He threw his spare shirt onto his only blanket and collected what tools he possessed and went back out to join his crazy friend.

Harriett was sitting on an upturned barrel swinging her legs when he came back out and as soon as she saw him she jumped down and walked out of the yard with Jimmy at her side.

Time and time again he promised himself that the next time she came up with some madcap idea he would flatly refuse to have anything to do with it but here he was, jobless, penniless and homeless sitting on the moor sharing her lunch and listening to her story but he had to admit it, he had never felt happier. Although he was shocked to hear about her being forced into marriage by The Fat Man, she assured him that this, Lord Planter, didn't want anything to do with her and he had gone off and she didn't know when he'd be back. Jimmy was back in the middle of it facing an uncertain future with his fearless little friend; life couldn't be better.

They came to the retaining wall and Harriett asked Jimmy to give her a boost up so she could get over the wall.

"What the devil for?" he asked.

"We can't let anyone know you're here until we get you settled in so we'll have to go in the back way. Anyway it cuts off a big corner."

He cupped his hands together. She placed her foot in them and he hoisted her up and over she went.

She turned to give Jimmy a hand up to find him already sitting on top of the wall. "How did you get up there?" she asked.

"There's hand and foot holds: easy," he grinned.

Following her through the wood they made their way to the cottages to face the farmhands.

"Hello again," Harriett shouted and waved.

"Back again, what can we do for you this time, my lady?" asked the same woman whom she had spoken to earlier in the day.

"Is there someone in charge that we can talk to?" asked Harriett.

"There's Mr Harrow, in the end cottage. He's just got back from the fields, you can go and talk to him." The woman jerked her thumb towards the end cottage.

"Thank you," Harriett said and they headed off to see Mr Harrow.

Harriett knocked on the door and waited. The door was opened by a large pleasant looking man clad in trousers and a loose-fitting, coarse linen shirt, open at the neck and sleeves rolled up above his elbows. He was rubbing his face with a piece of off white towelling.

"Mr Harrow?" asked Harriett.

"That's me," he replied, "and from the description Mrs Mason over there gave me, you must be the new lady of The Manor."

"I am and I would like you to meet Jimmy Hathaway. I've brought him to repair your cottages. He's a wonder with a hammer and nails and you'll find he can do most building jobs. One of the women told me earlier that there were spare building materials in the old barn. Can you show us?" Harriett asked.

Mr Harrow looked at Harriett and said, "Does his lordship know about this?"

"No, but no doubt he soon will when the servants up at the house find out about it. I don't think they will hold back on telling tales on me, but you might get a couple of the cottages repaired by then so I don't see you have anything to lose. Of course I will take the blame and tell him I insisted you allow Jimmy to do the repairs."

"I don't know about that. He can be very overbearing at times, and he left me in charge so, if I let you go around repairing something he hasn't authorized, I could find myself out of a job." Mr Harrow stroked his chin.

"If, Lord Planter dismisses you for trying to improve his property then he isn't worth working for. Jimmy has given up his job to come to help you out and make things better for you. Is this all the thanks he gets?" she wanted to know.

"Yes, maybe you are right, lass. Let me get my boots on and I'll be right with you." Mr Harrow vanished back inside his cottage.

"This way, lad. I hope you brought some tools because there's none here. Gave up your job did you? Can't have been a very good one." Mr Harrow looked across at Jimmy as they made their way to the old barn.

"You're right there, Mr Harrow," Jimmy agreed.

"This lot was rescued after being dumped on the moor. Old Mr Redman two miles over to the right knocked down all of his cottages so he could plough the land but he died, poor old sod, before he could do anything about it. The new owner wanted the stuff shifting, so me and some of the other men went over and brought it back here. We thought it might come in useful to repair our dilapidated cottages. It didn't cost us anything, only a few aches and pains with lugging it all over here but that's as far as we've got."

They stood in the doorway of the barn and looked at all the rubble: parts of thatched roofs, window frames with most of the panes of glass broken and piles of stone and wood.

"There's plenty to go at here but I think most of the glass seems to be broken." Jimmy walked amongst the building rubble checking this and testing that. "I'll be able to make use of all this other stuff though. I can repair the thatched roofs with this lot and these stones are in pretty good shape."

"Do you by any chance have an empty cottage for Jimmy to live in? If not I'm sure he wouldn't mind sleeping in here. It's a hundred times better than the rat-infested basement he was living in before." Harriett looked around the barn. The roof seemed to be intact and the door closed.

"There are two cottages empty at the moment but neither are fit to live in; he can take his pick," Mr Harrow said. "The two at the rear, they get the brunt of the weather, nearly all the roof is missing and the doors are off altogether. We had to take them off, because when the wind blew they were banging day and night but you'll find them inside. If you're handy with a hammer it won't take you long to put them back up. The cottages have been open to the elements and anything else that cared to wander in. You're welcome to have a look."

Harriett and Jimmy walked over to the two cottages. They were two storeys high and going up the narrow wooden stairway they came to a narrow landing with two bedrooms off, one larger than the other and both with sky showing overhead. Birds nested in what remained of the thatched roof and the windows held no glass. Going back downstairs there was a larger than average kitchen with a huge, deep, pot sink. There was a door leading into a pantry, two not so healthy looking chairs and a wooden table upside down boasting only three legs. The front room of the house consisted of a small open fireplace, a doorframe with no door and a window with no glass. The door was leaning against the wall.

"What do you think, Jimmy?" Harriett asked him.

"I think it's the most beautiful cottage I've ever seen. I can fix up the roof in no time. It won't take two minutes to get the door back on, there's plenty of wood in the barn and there were lots of iron nails I can retrieve. I can work on this in my own time when I've finished for the day. I'll get the farm workers' cottages started on and hope to get some of the repairs finished before Lord Hunter returns, and finds out about me and gets rid of me. That's what might happen when he finds out but I'm willing to take the chance; it's better than I had before. You know as well as I do, Harry, you can never second-guess the weather from one day to the next so the sooner I get started the better. Glass for the windows is going to be the only problem I can see at the moment. Just think a cottage of my own, even if it's only for a few days. It's a dream to treasure no matter how bad things get in the future. I'm going to have a word with Mr Harrow to find out which cottage needs to be repaired first. I'll see you around, Harry, a lot to do." And off he went.

Harriett made her way back to The Manor smiling to herself. She'd never seen Jimmy so happy or so confident. All his life he had been bullied and downtrodden because of his limp. The word cripple had followed him wherever he went and he had to take what job he could whenever it was offered. He usually worked for no pay but was provided with appalling lodgings like the one he'd just left and a meagre food ration. There was no wonder he thought the cottage was a palace.

Jimmy's mother had deserted him when he was thirteen years old and he'd had to fend for himself.

Harriett first met Jimmy when she was leaving church with her mother. It had been raining and the ground was thick with mud and Jimmy was rolling around in the mud with a boy twice his size; they were fighting and Jimmy was losing the battle. Harriett had pounced on the bigger boy and dragged him off by his hair, landing in the mud herself and finding she had then to fight the boy herself. She was used to fighting with her brother who was bigger than this boy and it wasn't long before she'd punched him in the nose making it bleed and he ran off crying. Harriett helped the mud-soaked youth to his feet and they both stood laughing at the sight of each other. That had been the start of their friendship.

The problem of the glass kept her awake that night, wondering how she could get some money to buy more glass when she suddenly remembered the advert in the milliner's window for a seamstress. Problem solved. She would have a walk into the village in the morning and see if the position was still available. She could sew; in fact she was a very good needlewoman. This made her think of the hours she'd spent altering her mother's old gowns to fit her and tears welled up and ran down her face. She couldn't express how much she missed her mother but she didn't have time to dwell on it. Harriett was so tired she was asleep before the last teardrop hit the pillow.

CHAPTER 4

Next morning, Harriett was up and dressed by the time Sally appeared. "Good morning, my lady. Mr Meanwood would like a word with you in the library."

"And who is Mr Meanwood?" Harriett asked her.

"Lord Planter's secretary, my lady," she replied.

"Very well, I will go down and see him and while I'm gone, would you be so kind as to have another packed lunch made up for me?" Harriett asked.

Harriett knocked on the library door and went in. Sitting behind Lord Planter's desk was a portly man of about five and thirty, hair plastered back, his face chubby making his beady little eyes look even smaller in appearance. His nose was a shade too long and his mouth a shade too wide with fat red lips. His cheeks were flushed and there were beads of sweat on his forehead. He took out a handkerchief and mopped his brow, and then wiped his lips.

"Lady Planter?" he asked.

"That is correct. You wanted to see me?"

"Lord Planter has instructed me to give you an allowance of one pound a month. I have written up an agreement for you to sign to say you have received the money. If you could just sign where I've marked it with a cross." Mr Meanwood dipped a quill in the ink and held it out to Harriett.

Harriett, having been well trained by her mother, ignored the offered quill and took hold of the paper instead. She intended to read the contents before she signed. The contents read:

> *I, Lady Planter do hereby receive the sum of £1 to be paid monthly until further notice.*
>
> *Signed:* ....*X*

"That is short and to the point," remarked Harriett taking the quill from him and signing the sheet. He eagerly took the sheet of paper from her and handed over the one-pound note. Harriett thanked him and left the room to find Sally waiting for her in the hall, holding her packed lunch.

"Thank you, I won't be in for the rest of the day," she told her.

Harriett cut across the lawn, through the wood and climbed over the boundary wall and set off for Welldeck at a leisurely pace. Arriving about nine o'clock she found the milliner's already open and the sign advertising for a seamstress still in the window. Entering the shop, the only person she could see was a very tall, thin woman arranging some very stylish hats on a display stand.

The woman looked up and, seeing a young woman modestly clad in a grey woollen dress, ignored her and went on with what she was doing. Harriett stood with her hands folded in front of her, waiting for the woman to finish what she was doing.

"Can I help you?" The woman looked down her long, narrow nose as she addressed Harriett.

"Yes, I have come to enquire about the seamstress's job you have advertised in the window," replied Harriett.

"Have you now, and can you sew?"

"I can."

"The last three women who came to apply for the job had difficulty in knowing which end of the needle to thread. You will have to give me a sample of your work before I can set you on. I have some very important customers and if they don't have the best, they will go elsewhere. Come with me." Turning, she led Harriett down a flight of wooden steps into a basement.

In the basement were rolls of materials in all different sizes and colours, set out on shelves along the walls. There was a long wooden table in the centre of the room. Sitting at this table under an iron chandelier hanging from the ceiling and lit by candles, was a young girl of about ten.

"Here, take this brim and attach it to the crown. Let me see a sample of your work." The lady handed Harriett two pieces of material and pointed to a drawer full of needles, pins and different coloured cottons.

Taking the offered goods, Harriett selected the cotton matching the colour of the material and set about attaching the brim to the head piece. She worked neatly but quickly while the woman stood over her. The little girl never looked up from what she was doing.

When Harriett had completed her task the woman took it from her and examined it. "Not bad, not bad at all. Very well,

I'll give you a week's trial and at the end of that week, I will pay you sixpence, providing you keep up with the work you are given. You may start right away. There is a lot to do. Jenny here will show you the ropes. I've got the shop to run but I'll be down to check up on you at intervals, so don't think you can sit on your backside all day. You may call me Madam Grace." She turned and went back upstairs.

"Are you Madam Grace's daughter?" Harriett asked the young girl.

"No, I just work here," was the reply.

"You seem a bit young to be in charge of all this," Harriett said kindly.

"I've been working here for the past four years. Madam Grace found me sleeping rough. My mother had left me to fend for myself and I survived by eating scraps of rotten food and begging. Madam Grace took me in and taught me to make hats and I've been here ever since," Jenny told her.

While they worked Jenny told Harriett she slept on a bed at the far end of the basement. Harriett found out that Jenny never went out and had never seen daylight since the day Madam Grace had taken her in. She was glad to be there. She was frightened Madam Grace would turn her out if she complained. Madam Grace had told her about men. Jenny didn't want to meet any men. They did bad things to you.

Harriett was shocked with the plight of Jenny who seemed to be happy and content to remain down in that basement feeling safe and fed. Something had to be done.

She was too exhausted to think by the time she reached The Manor and she went straight to her room, thankful for the cold meat and bread left for her at the side of the bed. She ate hungrily while she undressed.

By the end of the week Harriett decided to ask Madam Grace about Jenny, to see if she could get her at least to be allowed out of the basement for a while at the end of each working day. Harriett's eyes were sore and itchy from working in the semi-darkness and the candle smoke. It must be the same for Jenny. It couldn't be good for Jenny's eyesight alone, working in that light and those conditions.

On the last day of her first week Madam Grace was waiting in the shop for Harriett when she arrived at work. Her face was like thunder and she stood with her arms folded across her shapeless chest.

"*Out*, now! Get out of my shop and don't ever come back. How dare you work yourself into my business? You never told me you were Lord Planter's wife. If I had known that I would never have set you on. Here, there's your sixpence, now get out of my shop." Madam Grace held out a silver sixpence and Harriett took it.

"Who told you I was Lord Planter's wife?" Harriett wanted to know.

"He did, he came to the shop late last night and told me that if I didn't dismiss you he'd ruin me, and knowing him he would. All I can say is that he deserves you. He's arrogant and thinks he can make everyone do exactly as he says just because he has a title and money. He's a nasty, overbearing man and you're a little liar, going around without a wedding ring on, duping people. What did you expect to get out of it that's what I want to know?" the furious lady shouted. "Now get out of my shop, I don't want to see your face here again."

Harriett turned and left the shop and made her way back to The Manor. She jumped over the wall and stalked into the hall.

She was met by Wrenshaw who said, "Lord Planter is in his study. He would like a word with you."

"Does he indeed? No more than I want a word with him," Harriett told the shocked Wrenshaw.

Without knocking, Harriett opened the door and went in head held high, slamming the door behind her. "How dare you!" she demanded. "How dare you go to the milliner's and get me dismissed. How dare you! What right have you to tell me what I can do and what I can't do? You have no idea what you've done. You've committed a ten-year-old little girl to a life of drudgery down in that basement. It's a wonder she's not blind by now, being made to work God knows how many hours, seven days a week. You have done the child a terrible wrong. I was hoping to find a way to make things better for her. Why did you go and see Madam Grace? Why?"

"I don't know what the devil you're talking about. I know nothing about any ten-year-old girl," Lord Planter said. "I will not have my wife working in a milliner's shop. I have checked with Mr Meanwood and he tells me he has given you the ten pounds I instructed him to. He even showed me the receipt you signed to say you had received it."

Harriett paced the room; Mr Meanwood had given her one pound, not ten pounds. She had read the receipt before she had signed it. He must have added a nought afterwards. She'd had to live on her wits for as long as she could remember.

Harriett thought of how the house servants were well dressed and well fed whereas the farmhands lived in hovels, wore patched clothes and looked undernourished. Mr Harrow had said Lord Planter had not been down to the home farm for at least two years. It seemed strange that there was such a wide difference in the workers in Lord Planter's service. Mr

Meanwood had stolen nine pounds from her within the first few days of meeting her so how much had he stolen from the estate.

Lord Planter was puzzled at this strange behaviour. He watched Harriett pace to and fro and the concentration on her face told him she had forgotten all about him. He had never come across anyone like his new wife. He was used to people bowing and scraping to him, but on the few occasions they had met she had retaliated in the most unexpected ways. He was silent while he watched her pace the carpet.

She stopped pacing and faced him. "I am going to show you something, my lord. I don't want you to take this the wrong way but I think we need to get something straight so there's no mistaking where we stand with each other."

To his astonishment his wife started to unbutton the front of her dress. It wasn't often he was left speechless but this was one of them. Again, he hadn't expected her to start stripping off. It left him feeling disgusted with her. Did she think she could offer herself to him to get her own way?

But when Harriett had undone the last button at her waist she turned her back on him and dropped the dress down over her shoulders, leaving Lord Planter, once again, bereft of speech. He saw the red angry buckle marks across her back. He also saw old signs of previous beatings.

When she was sure Lord Planter had seen enough she pulled her dress back over her shoulders and began to re-button the front. "You said you would not have your wife going out to work. Well, the way I see it, I am not your wife. We are married, but I am not your wife. The night before we were married was the first time I knew of your existence. Gary Farnsworth told me I was going to marry you and I told him I

41

wasn't, hence the beating. In the end I gave in and to be truthful I would have married anyone just to get away from that existence. I didn't see what difference it would make to my life, being beaten by Gary Farnsworth or abused by a husband.

"You are blaming me for our marriage but it was you who got drunk and lost at cards. You might think you're clever, my lord, but Gary Farnsworth is crafty. If you hadn't had so little control over yourself as to be in such a drunken stupor, neither of us would be in the position we find ourselves in now, so don't you dare blame me for this predicament.

"I was poorly when we got married. My back hurt; I'd had nothing to eat; you sat me upon a horse when I'd never ridden a horse before in my life and to cap it all, all you men had hats on whilst I was left baking in the sun and all because you'd had too much to drink."

"I had no idea, but you're right, none of this is your fault. I'm sorry for causing you so much pain. I never dreamt you would get a beating because of it. I'm appalled," he admitted.

"I know you were unaware of the beating but it is of little consequence now. It is too late to alter things so we may as well rub along together as best we can. I say this because I think, my lord, you're being duped," she told him.

"Really!" he said in surprise, "and who may I ask is duping me?"

"Mr Meanwood."

"What makes you say that?"

"How long is it since you visited the home farm?"

"Two, maybe three years. There is no need for me to visit the farm; it's in good hands. Mr Harrow, the manager, is in charge and he's a very good man. He worked for my father, I know I can trust him."

"Yes, I've met Mr Harrow and I believe you can, but your faith in Mr Meanwood is misjudged. On the very day you left for wherever it was you went I decided to find my way to Welldeck and quite by chance I came upon your home farm. I must admit I was surprised to see your farm workers in such a dishevelled state compared to the healthy, well-dressed staff here at The Manor."

She went on to tell him of her lifelong friend who had, by necessity, to learn to survive by taking any job he could, and he had become very skilled in many areas. She told him of her conversation with Mr Harrow and that it was her that had pushed Mr Harrow into setting Jimmy to work and offering him one of the empty cottages.

"I was told you had brought your lover to live in one of my cottages down on the farm. I take it that this lifelong friend will be to whom the informant was referring?"

"My lover!" She laughed and her eye sparkled as they met his lordship's. "I would love to see Jimmy's face if he thought he had to be my lover. In fact I think he'd have a heart attack at the very thought. Was it Mr Meanwood that fed you this information?" she asked.

"It was," he admitted.

"And you believed him?"

"I had no reason to disbelieve him, and I could well have imagined it to be true. As you have already pointed out, we know nothing about each other. No doubt, in due course, you will hear things about me too. Some of the stories will be true, I've been no angel, but not everything you hear will hold water."

"In that case, my lord, shall we agree that neither of us will judge the other unless we know the information we receive about the other is proven?"

"Agreed," he nodded.

"Well, I may not be very worldly wise but I have had to live on my wits to keep ahead of Gary Farnsworth and, as you already know, he is a very crafty, sly snake in the grass so I am not that easy to fool. Mr Meanwood called me into the library and when I entered he was sitting behind your desk, which to me, showed little respect for your lordship. He handed me a piece of paper to sign, but before I signed it, I read it. The wording was that I was to receive one pound a month until further notice. I signed and he handed over the one-pound note. The first time I met this man and we did business together he stole nine pounds from me. He must have put a nought after the one-pound when I'd put my signature to the piece of paper. That and the state of your home farm, must, even to you set alarm bells ringing. I think he's fiddling the books. I think he's telling you he's spending money on the farm but only part of that money is going on the farm. I think he's lining his own pockets and by the state of the farm I think it's been going on for a long time. You don't have to take my word for it. Let us go down to the farm and you can take a look for yourself."

Lord Planter thought about what she had said. Surely he couldn't have been so ignorant as to what was happening on his estate, but it was true, he hadn't been down to the farm to check, he'd left it all to Mr Meanwood to sort out. Can what she'd said be true, about only signing for a one-pound note? Why would she lie? Especially since she had challenged him to go and see for himself the state of the farm. She had also mentioned this Jimmy openly and, in his opinion, innocently, he didn't think for one minute they were lovers. He stood up and going over to the fireplace he rang for the butler.

There was a knock on the door and Wrenshaw walked in.

"Ask Roy to join us would you, Wrenshaw?"

"Very well, my lord." Giving a slight bow from the waist he left the room.

"If, what you say is true, I've been very lax indeed. This is a sad state of affairs. Let's hope we can turn things around. You are full of surprises, Lady Planter. Why did you take it into your head to get a job? Being given, even a pound, must have seemed a lot of money to you, when I take it you never had any money from your father?"

"Mr Harrow heard of a neighbour of yours who had pulled down a row of cottages and wanted to get rid of the rubble. Because your cottages are in such a poor state of repair, your workers set about and brought the rubble back and stored it in the barn with the intention of using it to repair their own cottages. But then, when they had the rubble, there was no one with the skills to use it. That's why I went into town to get Jimmy. I knew he was dreadfully unhappy where he was so I thought it would kill two birds with one stone. By asking Jimmy to come and repair the cottages and rescue him from his present plight at the same time. There was no glass for the windows and I hit upon going out to work to get some money to buy some glass. I'd seen a notice in the milliner's window the previous day so off I went, got the job and that's how I came across poor little Jenny. Not that Jenny thinks she's poor. Madam Grace had taken her off the street. She's nothing but an unpaid slave," Harriett told him.

Before Lord Planter could say any more there was a knock on the door and Wrenshaw came in followed by a young man of about one and twenty being of very muscular build, blond hair and having a nose that wasn't quite straight.

"Thank you, Wrenshaw, that will be all."

"Very good, my lord." Wrenshaw closed the door.

"Roy, this is Lady Planter, my wife," introduced his lordship.

"Pleased to meet you, my lady." Roy gave a respectful nod.

"And I you," she replied.

"Do you still bare-knuckle fight down at the tavern, Roy?" Lord Planter asked the young man.

"I beg your pardon, my lord?" asked the startled young man.

"It's all right, Roy, I've known about your bare-knuckle fights for a while; in fact I've even won a few bob on you. Do you still teach young Tim the art of shall we say, self-defence?" Lord Planter wanted to know.

Harriett listened to this conversation in wonderment, she had heard of bare-knuckle fighting but she had never met anyone who could boast to having done it.

"You do bare-knuckle fighting, can I come and watch?" she asked him.

"*No*," replied her husband.

The light went out of her eyes as they met his and she was prompted to say, "Men have all the fun."

"That's as maybe but the answer is still no," Lord Planter assured her.

"Well?" he turned his attention back to Roy.

"I have been known to go a round or two with him, my lord, yes," replied Roy.

"Good, I might need your expertise later on today but right now I have another job for you. Do you think you can still do a bit of burglary?" his lordship wanted to know.

Roy scratched his chin. "Burglary, eh! It's been a while now, my lord, but I think I can still remember some of it. Who do you want me to burgle?"

Harriett's eyes shone. "You can burgle too?"

"Well, I don't want it to get around. I've been on the straight and narrow since I came to work for his lordship, those days are well behind me now," he told her.

"I won't tell anybody," she told him. "A bare-knuckle fighter and a burglar all in one," she said with admiration.

There was only the smallest smile on Lord Planter's lips as he continued, "You might not like what I am going to ask you to do, Roy, and you can say no if you would prefer not to do it."

"I know you wouldn't ask me to do anything you didn't think proper and I owe you more than I can repay so just ask away, my lord, I'll see what I can do."

"In a while I'm going to ask Mr Meanwood to accompany Lady Planter and myself to the home farm. While we're away I want you to go into Mr Meanwood's room and look for anything he has hidden, anything you might think belongs to me. You know all the hiding places where people keep their treasures, so anything he has tucked away I want you to put it in a bag and bring it down into the library when I send for you. Can you do that?" Lord Planter asked.

"Piece of cake, leave it to me," Roy grinned. "Been skimming the milk has he? Doesn't surprise me. If he's taken anything I'll find it."

"Don't you like him, Roy? I thought you all got on well together or so Mr Meanwood told me."

"Been pulling the wool over your eyes, has he? I suppose he can be very nice if he wants to. I'll be off then, this could be interesting." And off he went whistling.

Lord Planter stood up and going over to the fireplace he rang the bell once again. After a few seconds the door opened and Wrenshaw walked in. "Wrenshaw, have Mr Meanwood come down would you?"

"Very good, my lord," he replied and went back out.

Lord Planter looked at his wife and, for the second time, he had the feeling of having met her before, again it was only fleeting. He knew he had never met her before, if he had, he would have remembered. There was something about her that intrigued him. He liked looking at her and for some odd reason he liked being in her company.

She looked across at him and caught him looking at her and Lord Planter felt himself blush, something he hadn't done since he was in short trousers and was grateful when the door opened and Mr Meanwood walked in.

Mr Meanwood saw Harriett standing in the middle of the room while Lord Planter remained seated at his desk. "You wanted to see me, my lord?"

"Yes, come in, Trevor, and sit down. It seems a couple of problems have arisen but I'm sure you will have an explanation for them." Lord Planter pointed to the hard-backed chair on the opposite side of his desk.

Mr Meanwood moved slowly to the chair and sat down. He felt the room closing in on him. Glancing at Lady Planter standing upright and confident, then meeting Lord Planter's eyes his hands began to sweat and he wiped them on his trousers. Mr Meanwood was the first to glance away.

"Lady Planter informs me, Trevor, that you only paid her one pound and not the ten pounds you were instructed to give her. Is that right?" asked his lordship.

"Certainly not, my lord, you've seen the receipt she signed. Is she trying to say I've cheated her out of some money?" he asked.

"She is, yes, and I must admit, Trevor, her explanation holds water. She says you added a zero to the amount of money she signed for, after the event," he informed him.

"Whose word would you rather believe, my lord, a trusted employee or, shall I say, that of a scheming woman?" Mr Meanwood cast Harriett a contemptuous look.

"Are you referring to my wife when you say a scheming woman?" Lord Planter asked.

"We all know how she came to be your wife, my lord. I don't think she is to be trusted," came the reply.

"You all know nothing of the kind, Trevor. How Lady Planter came to be my wife is none of your business or anyone else's and I wish you to bear that in mind. When you address Lady Planter you will do so with the respect she deserves. Is that understood?" Lord Planter's voice was edged with steel.

"As you wish, my lord." He inclined his head slightly.

"Another thing my wife has accused you of, Trevor, is letting the home farm go to rack and ruin. Is that correct?" Lord Planter held Mr Meanwood's panic-stricken gaze.

"How can she know anything of the home farm, she's just a woman and she hasn't been here long enough to know anything about the farm," replied the accused.

"Well, there's no time like the present. We'll all go down to the farm and have a look shall we?" His lordship stood up and indicated for Mr Meanwood to do the same.

Mr Meanwood stayed seated. "I'm sure there's no need for us all to go, my lord. I'll wait here for your return and I know you will be ready with an apology for me when you get back." Lord Planter took three large strides, grabbed Mr Meanwood by the scruff of his neck and marched him to the door.

Harriett had to run to keep up with Lord Planter's long quick strides. Mr Meanwood complained all the way.

Harriett was at a loss about Lord Planter's replies to Mr Meanwood's denial and his defence of her. It was something she hadn't expected. As she ran by his side her heart sank. Was this to be the end of Jimmy's dream? What was he going to do if Lord Planter threw him off his land? It was her fault he'd left his last job, another mess she'd landed him in, poor Jimmy. She must think of something to keep him in a job. She couldn't desert him. They had been friends for too long.

They reached the farm and Mr Harrow, having seen them approaching, came forward to greet them. "Lord Planter, it's good to see you, my lord."

"It would seem I have been neglecting my duties, Mr Harrow, will you show us round?"

Lord Planter let go of Mr Meanwood's collar and there was nothing he could do but follow the other two gentlemen around the neglected farm, cottages and barns. They looked in the barn housing all the rubble and found Jimmy hard at work pulling nails out of a piece of timber.

"This is Jimmy, my lord. Lady Planter brought him here to repair the cottages and a fine job he's been doing too." Mr Harrow introduced Jimmy.

"I heard you'd been drafted in, Jimmy," grinned Lord Planter shaking the young man's hand.

"Yes, a force to be reckoned with our Harry, but I didn't need much persuading, my lord. Anything was better than what I was doing." He grinned back at his lordship and a bond was formed between them.

Harriett decided she would wait with the woman she had spoken to on finding herself on the home farm. She found out her name was Mrs Brown. Her husband was the herdsman and they had four children. Sarah, her eldest, was seventeen, then there was Rose, fifteen, then came Louisa, thirteen, and last but not least young Ben, who was ten and the apple of his father's eye. She told Harriett her husband had given up on having a son after three girls and when Ben was born, he was over the moon. They were still talking when the gentlemen returned. Glancing at Lord Planter, Harriett could read nothing from his face and Mr Meanwood seemed to have shrunk in size. Maybe it's because his head was nearly on his chest, she thought.

"Thank you, Mr Harrow. I know my father called you Will. Is it all right if I do the same?" his lordship asked.

"I would deem it an honour, my lord. Will, it is."

"Good. Then, Will, if you and Jimmy could come up to the house at nine o'clock in the morning, we have things to discuss."

"Very good, my lord," confirmed a pleased Mr Harrow.

Lord and Lady Planter with Mr Meanwood between them made their way back to The Manor in silence. Harriett took another glance over at his lordship and found him looking at her. She felt her cheeks burn and her heart miss a beat as their eyes met and she looked away in confusion. The tiniest smile appeared on his lordship's lips. She's delightful he thought.

Back in the library Lord Planter told Mr Meanwood to sit down then he rang the bell and asked Wrenshaw to have Roy join them.

A knock at the door brought Roy into the room carrying what looked very much like a pillowcase bulging at the seams. He met Lord Planter's eyes and with a satisfied grin, gave a cheeky nod.

"While we were out, Mr Meanwood, I instructed Roy to go through your room and bring anything here that he might think belongs to me and, by the look of that sack, he might have hit upon a few objects," Lord Planter said.

"You've been through my things? You had no right to do so, they are my things how dare you. I'll have the constabulary on you." Mr Meanwood started to stand up but Roy pushed him back down.

"Empty the content onto the desk, Roy. Let's see what you have found," Lord Planter told his servant.

Enjoying himself more than he cared to admit, Roy turned the sack upside down and shook the contents onto the desktop. A number of silver items fell out along with a duelling pistol, an expensive leather-bound address book, and several rolls of bank notes.

"They're mine," shouted a distraught Mr Meanwood. "You can't prove otherwise."

"Oh, I think I can. This address book for instance," said Lord Planter, holding up the book, "was given to me by Lord Tandleson, I'm sure he'll be able to confirm it. It seems you have been taking what is not yours Mr Meanwood and over a long period. What else do you have that belongs to me?"

"Nothing, there's nothing more." Mr Meanwood hung his head.

"I blame myself for allowing you to do such a thing. I had put my trust in you and it was obviously misguided. Roy is going to go back up to your room with you while you pack your bags, just to make sure you put nothing in that doesn't belong to you. Then he's going to drive you into Welldeck and drop you off and it had better be the last time I set eyes on you. The further away you go the better it will be for you. I hope I make myself clear? You are lucky I don't set the Peelers on you, now get out."

Lord Planter nodded to Roy.

"All right you light-fingered rogue, off we go and don't even think about trying to run off. I'm quicker than you and I also pack quite a punch." Roy grabbed Mr Meanwood by the arm and led him away.

Harriett looked at Lord Planter and asked, "Did you know Roy was a thief when you hired him?"

"I did, I came home one night and found him about to break into The Manor. He tried to run off but I caught him and found out he was an orphan, and he too has had to live on his wits from an early age, a bit like your Jimmy really. I gave him a job in the stables and when old Mr Watson retired Roy took over and now he runs the stables. He's an excellent groom. He handles the horses better than anyone I've ever employed. It could be that they are the first things in his life he has ever had any love for and I think they sense it. Things worked out to my advantage when I hired Roy. One or two of the other estate owners around here have tried to poach him, but he remains loyal and I can't ask for more than that," he told her.

"About Jimmy, Lord Planter – it was my fault he left his last employment. Could you at least keep him on until he finds somewhere else to work?" Harriett looked across the room at his lordship.

"He's coming to see me in the morning with Will. We need to sort a few things out, we'll settle everything then," he told her.

She gave him a small curtsey and left the room.

CHAPTER 5

Will and Jimmy were shown into the library and asked to sit on the two chairs placed on the opposite side of the desk to where Lord Planter sat.

"Good morning," he greeted them. "Now, Will, tell me what needs to be done to get the farm back on its feet."

"Well, my lord, pretty much everything really. Mr Meanwood kept the livestock down to the minimum and we only got half the corn we need to plant for a good harvest. We could do with some more chickens and a couple of cockerels and maybe some ducks to produce eggs. Mrs Brown will look after them with the help of her children. There's a farmers' market on at Welldeck on Thursday. Might be some cows and a bull worth buying and maybe a carthorse to help pull the plough. If you're going to get the farm working you might be able to buy some sheep as well and some goats, their milk makes good cheese. That's just for starters. Jimmy has made a good start on the cottages but as you know the weather can turn at the drop of a hat. There are a lot of repairs still to be done before winter comes. You've seen the building materials we rescued from old Harrison so that's going to save you some money, my lord. The only thing there seems to be a shortage of is glass for the broken windows. You did ask, I'm afraid it's going to cost rather a lot of money to set things right and get the farm up and running again," Will told him.

"After seeing the sorry state of affairs at the farm, Will, I can well believe it. First though, Jimmy, I would like to offer you employment but you must work under Will. He will set you the jobs he wants doing. Harriett tells me you're a jack-of-all-trades and by the look of things we're going to put you to good use. I believe you have already been allotted a cottage, if that's what you can call it in the state it's in, but I'm sure you'll be able to get it back to comfortable living accommodation."

"You're setting me on? I can't believe it. I'd give my left arm to stay here, and my own cottage as well. This is what dreams are made of. Thank you, my lord; I'd love to work under Will. I've only known him for a few days but we're already good friends," Jimmy beamed.

"Good, then that's settled, but keep your left arm, you're going to need it," Lord Planter smiled. "What I'm going to tell you now is confidential so I'm asking both of you to keep this under your hats because it makes me look rather foolish. Mr Meanwood has been skimming money off me for the last couple of years. I have no excuse; it's my own fault. It took my wife to open my eyes to the deception but fortunately most of the money has been retrieved. He'd been hoarding it and it's now back in my possession. The money I thought was going into the farm can now be ploughed back into it."

Lord Planter opened the top drawer of his desk and took out three rolls of notes; one he passed to Jimmy.

"That, Jimmy, should pay for glass for the cottages, if not, just let me know." The other two rolls he passed to Will, adding, "That should buy some chickens and ducks and anything else you might need. You say there's a farmers' market on Thursday. Shall we set off early and see what they have on sale? I'll pick you up at the gate around seven a.m.," he said.

"Thank goodness you've come to your senses at last, my lord, if you don't mind me saying so," grinned Will.

"Too late to say if I did mind, Will. You've already said it." Lord Planter smiled.

Jimmy stood up, itching to go so he could sort out his little cottage, his own little cottage.

Harriett was sitting at the bottom of the stairs hugging her knees waiting for Will and Jimmy to come into the hall. She sprung to her feet when the library door opened, holding onto the banister for support, dreading the worst.

Jimmy saw her and gave her a broad grin. "What's the long face for, Harry? Sorry, I should say, Lady Planter, now I'm an employee of yours, and guess what, the cottage is mine. Can't stop chatting, loads to do." But before he left he gave her a big hug and whispered in her ear, "Don't forget where I live, Harry." He kissed the top of her head and left.

Lord Planter stood in the doorway watching these proceedings and Harriett meeting him in the eye mouthed, "Thank you."

His lordship smiled and mouthed back, "No, thank you."

Not wanting his lordship to see the tears welling up in her eyes she walked across the hall and out into the warm sunshine. She was so pleased for Jimmy. It was about time he had a bit of luck in his life but there was also sadness too. Harriett knew that although they would always be friends their circumstances had changed and it would never be the same between them again. She carried on walking and made her way into the wood. She felt the need of a bit of peace and quiet and walking through the majestic trees with shafts of sunlight shining down, she felt all the tension easing away.

Harriett hadn't gone very far when she felt a tight arm around her waist and she let out a scream. Gary Farnsworth's ugly face was grinning at her when she turned her head to see who had grabbed her. Standing next to him was Ronald. "Told you it wouldn't be the last time we saw you, my stuck up little sister," he said.

"Let me go, you brute." Harriett kicked him in the shin and he let her go but not before giving her a hefty push in the back and sending her flying headlong along the rough grass.

Harriett stood up and brushed down her dress. "What do you want?" she demanded. "You'll get nothing from me and if Lord Planter knows you're roaming his land, I hope he sets the Peelers on you both and they lock you up and throw away the key."

"Now I think the last thing his lordship needs is his father-in-law locked up. I want you to tell him that Ronald and I are coming to see him tonight at seven o'clock. I'm sure he'll be very generous to his starving relations. You just tell him to expect us this evening, my pretty." Ronald gave her a quick punch on the arm and laughing they walked away.

That evening Sally came into her room and told her from now on she was to eat with his lordship downstairs and that dinner was at six o'clock in the dining room.

During dinner Harriett played with her food, something she had not done since going to live at The Manor. Lord Planter knew there was something on her mind but he left her to get round to telling him in her own good time. He saw her keep looking at her left hand and he'd also noticed she held her fork at an odd angle so he decided to help her out. "What's wrong with your hand?" he asked.

"It's nothing," she replied, placing it on her lap under the table.

He stood up and advanced towards her. Taking her left wrist he turned her hand over and saw a nasty graze covering her upturned palm. "How did you get this?" he demanded.

Harriett knew she had to tell Lord Planter that he was going to have visitors after dinner but she just didn't know how to begin.

"Well, I'm waiting!" he said taking hold of her hand and gently moving it up and down and from side to side making sure it wasn't broken. "What happened, Harriett?"

"The Fat Man and his Toad are coming to see you tonight," she blurted out.

He let go of her hand and went and sat back at the table. "The Fat Man and his Toad, now that conjures up a picture. Does this Fat Man have a name?" he asked.

"Gary Farnsworth and Ronald." She hung her head.

"Your father and brother," he continued, looking at her. "Did he do that to your hand?"

"I was walking in the wood and he jumped out at me and when I kicked him in the shin he pushed me and I fell down. I put my hand out to save myself and grazed it along the grass. He's not my father and Ronald is only my stepbrother. The Fat Man and his Toad are what my mother and I called them. They are coming here tonight to try and extract money from you. Please don't give them any. This is why he made me marry you. He thinks he will be able to get money from you.

Blackmail you into giving him money. I hate him and his toad, please Lord Planter, don't give them a penny," Harry begged.

"There's no need to get yourself in such a state, Harriett. There's no way I'd give either of them anything, even if you had begged me to do so. I am well aware of why he wanted me to marry you but I think he will find it has backfired on him. He's not your father you say, then who is your father?" he wanted to know.

"I don't know. I didn't know until my mother was taken ill. She told me that The Fat Man wasn't my father but she wouldn't tell me who is. She said he would most likely be married with children of his own and he never knew about me so she wouldn't tell me." She went on to explain to him how her mother became married to Gary Farnsworth.

The more Lord Planter heard about this man the more he disliked him. Something had to be done about him. He would not have him frightening his wife ever again or harming her in any way. Lord Planter rang the bell and waited for Wrenshaw.

At just turned seven o'clock, Wrenshaw answered the front door and The Fat Man and his Toad were shown into the library. "Lord Planter will be with you directly." He gave a slight nod and closed the door on them.

They both looked around the expensively decorated room, noting highly embellished silver ornaments and exquisite porcelains, but then Ronald noticed a young man sitting at his leisure in one of the plush leather armchairs.

"Who the devil are you?" demanded Ronald.

"The name's Roy. I've been asked to keep an eye on you two, make sure you don't put anything in your pockets that doesn't belong to you. By the way you've been eyeing things up I guess it's been a good decision." Roy grinned.

"Where's his lordship?" asked The Toad.

"Having his dinner with his wife. Do you expect them to leave their dinner and come to see what you two are after especially since you invited yourselves?" Roy was enjoying himself immensely.

It was half an hour before Lord Planter made an appearance with Harriett at his side.

"You wanted to see me?" Lord Planter asked as Roy left the room.

"I did indeed, my lord. I'm pleased my little Harry told you to expect us." He wrung his hands together. "The thing is, my lord, we have had the misfortune to find ourselves in the clutches of the money lenders and if we don't repay the money we owe they will have us thrown into jail. I'm sure your lordship can do without the humiliation of having your father-in-law in jail."

"I am informed by my wife that you are not her father so therefore you are not my father-in-law, and for the way you have treated her and her mother I think jail is the best place for you," Lord Planter replied.

"You told him that! You sneak, you nasty tale telling little sneak." Ronald advanced towards Harriett but, before he had taken more than two steps, Lord Planter hit him squarely on the chin sending him reeling backwards onto the floor.

Harriett, much impressed with this turn of events went across to the moaning Toad and kicked him as hard as she could in the ribs. Ronald made a move to catch her ankle but Harriett flew back and stood behind his lordship.

"There's no way I will pay off any of your debts. I would see you jailed first and I do not take kindly to being blackmailed. Nor do I appreciate you coming onto my land uninvited but, even more than that, I have a strong aversion to you manhandling my wife. I have seen the belt marks to her back and also her grazed hand from you pushing her to the ground. As a result of these facts I wish to be rid of you both, so here is what I am prepared to do for you.

"There is a ship sailing for Australia at four o'clock in the morning. I will pay for you and your son to have a cabin and the captain will receive a hundred pounds to give to you once you are out at sea. This will give you a start when you reach Australia. I have a rig waiting to take you both to Berkwash right now and my groom, whom you have already met, will stay with you until you are aboard ship and well underway before he returns. This way you will dodge your creditors and my wife will be rid of you once and for all. Take it or leave it."

"Australia, if you think you can get rid of us that easy, you have another thing coming," Ronald said, still gingerly feeling his chin.

"Then wait for the gull catchers to catch up with you. I will instruct my gamekeepers if they ever see you again on my land, they are to shoot first and ask questions later. Is that understood?" his lordship asked. "It is of little consequence to me. Whatever you do, I don't expect to see you again."

"A hundred pounds you say. All right give us the hundred pounds and we'll be off," said The Fat Man.

"My man, Roy, has the hundred pounds and he is instructed to give it to the captain of the ship along with a letter of explanation. You will get the money when you can no longer see dry land," Lord Planter informed them.

"Very well, we don't seem to have much choice do we?" said The Fat Man.

Lord Planter rang the bell and Wrenshaw was asked to tell Roy to go in.

Silence hung heavily in the room until Roy appeared.

"Is everything ready for the journey, Roy? You have the money and the letter? Does Tim know what to do?" asked Lord Planter.

"Everything is in hand, my lord. The rig is outside with Tim at the reins," Roy told him.

"Good, do you think these two will be a problem?" he asked Roy.

Roy looked both men up and down, then gave a cheeky grin. "No problem at all, my lord, we'll have them aboard ship and on their way in no time. This way if you please." Roy stood aside and indicated the door.

"Are you really sending them to Australia?" Harriett asked when they had gone.

"I am. When Lord Tandleson and I were in the army we made a number of friends amongst the navy captains who have since gone onto pilot private cargo ships. I happen to know Captain Grey is sailing for Australia in the early hours of tomorrow, so the timing is perfect. You heard me tell them, I've written a letter to the captain explaining the circumstances and why they are on their way to Australia and also explained the hundred pounds. If The Fat Man and his Toad think they are in for an easy passage they are very much mistaken. The Fat Man thinks he's very clever but these sailors know how to look after themselves and, once The Fat Man gets his hand on the hundred pounds, it won't take long for the sailors to take it from him. All legitimate I must add. They know about playing cards, there's nothing else for them to do and there will be plenty of time for them to part The Fat Man from his money. Captain Grey might even make them work their passage. I forgot to send some money to pay for their cabin so I think they will get what they deserve." Lord Planter smiled down at her.

"Oh I do hope so. I hope they throw them both over the side of the ship in the middle of the ocean and they get eaten by a whale who spits out their eyeballs and they have to watch other fish coming and eating their eyeballs and spitting them out for ever and ever," Harriett said with feeling and without taking a breath.

Lord Planter looked down at her and could not help but laugh out loud. "Remind me not to cross you, I dread to think what fate you'd concoct up for me." His eyes sparkled.

"If you don't mind me saying so, my lord, that was the best right hook I've ever seen. I wish it had been me that punched Ronald on the chin. But knowing The Fat Man he'll be planning something even now. I hope Roy will be all righ., I wouldn't put it past those two to set about Roy and Tim, steal the hundred pounds and head back here. I don't think The Fat Man had any intention of going to Australia. He agreed to the scheme too easily; you don't know him as I do. I think he only agreed to go to get his hands on the money," Harriett told him.

"If I know Roy, he'll be willing them to try something on. Roy is one of the best bare-knuckle fighters I've seen and he's been training Tim in the art, so I know who will come off worst if they try to outwit Roy. They'll be on their way to Australia early in the morning so you won't have to worry about them again," he told her.

She looked up at him and said, "I think my mother would have approved of you."

"Thank you, I feel I might have approved of your mother too. She certainly did an excellent job of bringing you up under extreme conditions," he replied.

"Yes she did. My only regret is that she didn't live to see you pack them off to the other side of the world. It was very neatly done, sir."

"I aim to please." He smiled. "Now let me see that hand of yours."

"It's nothing; I've bathed it and cleaned it out. I've had worse things happen to me, I'm a quick healer," she told him.

Ignoring her protest he held out his hand and she placed hers in it, palm up. He scrutinized the graze and seemed happy with it. "It looks nice and clean but keep an eye on it, make sure it doesn't get infected."

Harriett's heart was beating so rapidly she could hardly breathe. She withdrew her hand and said, "Thank you I will. It's my wrist that hurts more than the graze; it took all my weight when I fell."

"It's not broken but you might have sprained it. It should be all right in a few days." His eyes met hers and she felt her cheeks turning pink and found it hard to look away.

The weather had started to turn colder and heading nowhere in particular her thoughts began to wander. She tried to understand the effect Lord Planter had on her. These feelings were all new to her, the beating heart, the churning in her stomach when she saw him and the feeling of belonging when she was in the same room as him. She knew she would never really belong at The Manor but at least they were getting along nicely and his consideration for her was paramount: he couldn't do enough for her.

She found herself heading towards Welldeck and her daydreaming came to an end when, on the outskirts of the town she heard loud laughter coming from a crowd gathered up ahead. Her curiosity took her to the edge of the crowd and there she saw a large stationary horse-drawn coach.

An elegantly dressed lady was standing on the steps of the coach pointing a whip at a negro who was standing by the side of the coach, naked apart from a loin cloth covering his nether regions. He held his head high and his hands were folded in front of him.

"Come on now, isn't anybody going to buy him? He's a good worker. Make me an offer, the first person to make an offer gets him," the elegant lady shouted.

The crowd roared with laughter but Harriett was shocked at such degrading behaviour towards another human being. If she had some money, she would buy him. Then she remembered the sixpence Madam Grace had given her. Feeling in her cloak pocket she found the coin and holding it up she said, "I will buy the negro, here's sixpence."

"Sold to the lady for sixpence." The lady held out her hand and Harriett gave her the money. "Farewell, everybody!" The lady disappeared inside the coach and off it went.

The crowd began to disperse, the show was over and Harriett found herself standing alone with a naked negro. She took off her cloak and handed it to him. He was standing exactly where he was staring straight ahead. He made no move to take it. "Here, put this round your shoulders, you must be freezing. What a horrible woman. I think you're well rid of her only I haven't the foggiest idea what to do with you." Noticing he had no shoes on she bent down and took off her boots, then her thick woollen socks and after replacing her boots she held out the socks to him. "Look, I can understand your reluctance but you have nowhere else to go. I have no idea what I'm going to do with you. Just put on the cloak and the socks, we have a trek over the moors before we get to The Manor. Lord Planter will know what's best for you."

Without a word the negro took the cloak and pulled it round his body, then, he placed the socks on his feet. They were somewhat on the small side for him but they were better than nothing.

Harriett set off back towards The Manor with the negro following her. She was in another fix but there was no way she could have left the poor man to suffer any more humiliation. Harriett's heart sank at the thought of telling Lord Planter but, it was too late now, once again she had let her heart rule her head.

While Harriett was busy buying her negro, Lord Planter had returned home from Welldeck farmers' market with Will, but there had been nothing worth buying besides some hens and ducks. He went into the library and had just finished taking off his jacket and boots and settled down with his feet up on the couch and a glass of port in his hand when the door opened and in strolled Lord Tandleson, his best friend.

"Just been to Berkwash to see Captain Lally; he sails for Africa at two in the morning. He sends his best wishes and all that. Thought I'd just drop by and see how you're coping with the new wife. You've not been seen these past couple of months, is everything all right?" Lord Tandleson asked his friend.

"Tandy, how wonderful to see you. Grab yourself a port and make yourself comfortable. I've a lot to tell you. You'll never believe it, I still can't believe it myself." Lord Planter pointed in the direction of the port.

"Don't mind if I do, want a top up?" he asked.

"Why not, in fact bring the decanter over Tandy, save us jumping up for a refill."

Tandy carried over the decanter and his glass and sat in a tall comfy leather chair opposite his lordship. "Well off you go, Nick my boy, I'm all ears." He raised his glass before taking a drink.

"Tandy, I'm in love," Nick told his friend.

"The devil you are," replied a shocked Tandy.

"You've no idea what's happened to me in the last couple of months Tandy. I've just got back from a farmers' market, tramped up and down trying to find a bull but without success, hence the boots off, my feet are killing me." Nick indicated a raised bootless foot.

"Devil take your feet, Nick, what's this about being in love? Don't believe it, not you, confirmed bachelor if ever there was one, never been in love in your life. Had too much port, my good fellow? I should stay off it if I were you," advised Tandy.

"No, it's true, Tandy. I've fallen head over heels in love and I've never had so much fun in my life, except for the aching feet of course. I've been down at the home farm trying to get things back to normal but let me start at the beginning…" And so Lord Nicholas Planter proceeded to tell his best friend of the events since they had last met.

When Nick had finished his story, Tandy said, "You sent your father-in-law to Australia? That's a bit extreme isn't it?"

"Not with a father-in-law like mine, but as I told you, Tandy, The Fat Man, as she calls him, isn't her father.

"If The Fat Man's not her father, who is?" asked Tandy.

"She has no idea, her mother wouldn't tell her. But at least I haven't got that monster as a father-in-law and, if Harriett had her way, he would be thrown over the side of the ship, eaten by a whale and his eyeballs spat back out to keep watching fish coming and eating them and then being spat out for ever and ever." Nick's eyes danced as they met Tandy's shocked gaze.

"You're having me on," Tandy said.

"No, it's true, Tandy, every word I've told you. Life has become so exciting I never know what's going to happen next. I never know what she's going to come out with and her innocence is appealing, her honesty and generosity a breath of fresh air. I never thought I'd fall in love but, I am so content, Tandy, content to walk down to the home farm and get involved, to take interest in the estate instead of leaving it all to the servants. She's saved me thousands of pounds, which that conniving Meanwood, had stolen from me: around five thousand pounds. That's the amount Roy recovered from his bedroom all rolled up and hidden under the floorboards, to say nothing of the silver he'd stolen. It's all down to Harriett and she has asked for nothing for herself.

"Just wait until you see her again, Tandy, now she's not ill. She's very beautiful and I'm happy just to be in the same room as her. She sits and reads sometimes after we've had dinner and I sit and watch her, she fascinates me. All these scrapes she gets into, she openly admits them, but it's the way that she comes out with it. I know exactly when something is going on; she goes all around the houses to get to the front door." Nick's eyes sparkled with mischief.

"Well I'm damned if I can see the attraction in going to the farmers' market and ending up with aching feet. Best let the

69

servants do it, that's what I say. And you enjoy sitting and watching someone read. I think you've had too much sun, dear boy," Tandy said dubiously. "As for being in love, it will soon wear off, bound to."

"I hope not, I rather like it," Nick told him.

"What does she say about it?" Tandy asked.

"She doesn't know. I'm treading carefully; she didn't want to marry me in the first place. I don't want to scare her off, she's only nineteen and I'm nearly thirty. I'm just short of ten years her senior," Nick said. "She's had a bad experience with the Fat Man and his Toad, the Toad being her stepbrother of course. I'm giving her time and I'm hoping against hope she will at

After our first showdown regarding her going out to work, I went to see this Madam Grace and made enquires about the child she had working for her and found Harriett was right. This young girl was very distrustful of me. She cowed and hid behind Madam Grace, God knows what she's been told about men. Anyway I paid Madam Grace twenty pounds for the girl and took her away screaming and kicking into the coach to bring her to The Manor. My intentions were to bring her to Harriett, but the state the child was in I thought it best to take her to the convent, to Mother Mary Joan. That's where she is now. I'm hoping the nuns can help her. Mother Mary Joan is going to write to me and let me know of her progress, then I'll take Harriett to see her and hope that she approves of what I've done."

"My, you have been busy, Nicky my boy, no wonder your feet hurt. Sounds like they haven't had much rest in the past couple of months," Tandy said.

"You don't know the half of it, Tandy. I've had the time of my life, one thing after another," Nicky grinned.

Harriett, arriving at The Manor with her negro, went round the side of the building and into the kitchen. She'd decided, on her way home, that she would feed him first then go and see Lord Planter. She knew she would have to go and see him straight away because if she didn't, the servants would tell him before she had time to concoct up a story, so she decided the truth would be best.

Things didn't go quite to plan. As soon as she walked into the kitchen Mrs Raynor started to scream and shout, "Take him out of my kitchen, we'll all be eaten alive," putting her hands to her ample bosom and collapsing on a chair.

"Don't be ridiculous, Mrs Raynor, the poor man's starving, he needs food. If you won't find him something to eat, then I will," Harriett told her.

"You're not to use my plates, we'll all end up poisoned. Take him out of here," Mrs Raynor demanded.

"I'll do no such thing," said Harriett and she proceeded to cut some bread and butter onto a plate, added some cold meats and poured the negro a glass of milk.

"Oh my, what will you do next?" Mrs Raynor never took her eyes off the negro.

The other servants went to stand behind Mrs Raynor. They watched in silence as the negro ate his repast and drank his milk. When he had finished Harriett motioned him to follow her. She took him upstairs and put him in the spare room next door to the master bedroom.

CHAPTER 6

The soft tap on the library door interrupted the two gentlemen's conversation. Turning their heads they saw the door open slowly and Harriett squeeze through into the room, closing the door quietly behind her.

Lord Planter's eyes sparkled as they met his friend's, then both their gazes turned on the lady in the grey woollen dress. Harriett walked slowly and silently into the centre of the room, head downcast. She finally glanced up to see Lord Planter looking at her over the top of the couch and, feeling herself blush, she made her way round to the front to face him. She gave a little curtsey and said in a quiet voice, "Lord Planter."

Lord Planter inclined his head and said, "Lady Planter."

Harriett felt her face burn and was pushed into saying, "I wish you wouldn't call me that, it puts me off."

"Beg pardon, what would you like me to call you?" he asked.

"Harry will do, everyone calls me Harry."

"Well, Lady Planter, I'm not everyone, so if you want me to call you something other than Lady Planter, it will have to be either Harriett or Hetty. Which would you prefer?" he asked.

"Hetty," she replied.

"Hetty it will be, but only if you call me Nicky. Agreed?" he asked.

"I don't feel very comfortable with that," she told him.

"Nevertheless, if I'm to call you Hetty then I would like you to call me Nicky. I'm sure you'll soon get used to it."

"Very well, but now you've made me forget what I came to tell you," she said all flustered.

"Whilst you're remembering, say hello to Lord Tandleson." He indicated his head in Tandy's direction. "Do you remember him?"

"Yes, I have a vague recollection, you are the gentleman that helped me onto that huge horse. I beg your pardon, sir, I did not know Lor... er, Nicky, had a visitor." She gave him a neat curtsey.

"Don't mind me, Hetty, I'm practically one of the family. You certainly look better than the last time I saw you," he approved.

"Yes, Lor... er Nicky has been taking good care of me," she told him.

"Well if you have things to discuss with Lor...er Nicky, I'll make myself scarce and go and pester Mrs Raynor. I'm devilishly hungry." He made to stand up.

At the mention of Mrs Raynor, Harriett remembered the state she had left her in and, not wanting Lord Tandleson to find himself at the end of the irate Mrs Raynor's tongue, she said, "No, please stay, Lord Tandleson. You will no doubt hear about this in due course so, as Lor... er Nicky's friend you might as well hear it from the horse's mouth."

Tandy looked across at Nicky and saw him nod, so he sat back down and said, "All my friends call me Tandy."

"Thank you, Tandy, then so will I." She looked back at Nicky and said, "You're not going to like this, I'm afraid. In fact, there are two things you're not going to like, one worse than the other."

She waited for comment from Nicky, when none came, she continued, "You know when I first came here and I went to work for Madam Grace and you didn't like it?"

"I remember," he told her.

"Well she gave me sixpence for the work I'd done before you got me dismissed." Again she looked at him and waited for any comment. When none came she carried on, "I've spent it."

Tandy sat intrigued looking from one to the other and he had to admit there was something between them. They seemed to complement each other.

"It was yours to spend on anything you wished," he told her.

"Yes, but that's just it. You're not going to like what I spent it on," she told him.

Nicky sat thinking of things that he wouldn't like for sixpence. After seeing the prices at the farmers' market he couldn't think of a single thing. He sat and waited for her to continue.

Tandy could stand it no longer, and he asked, "What the devil have you bought, Hetty?"

Harriett glanced quickly at him then back at Nicky. "I've bought a man," she told them both.

Tandy was just taking a sip of his port and ended up having a coughing fit. "Peg pardon," he spluttered. "Went down the wrong way."

"I see, and what do you intend to do with this man?" Nicky asked her.

"That's the rub. I've no idea, that's why I brought him to you. I thought you might know what to do with him," she told him.

This was too much for Tandy. He burst out laughing and had to wipe the tears from his eyes. "Sorry, Hetty, that was the last thing I expected to hear. You bought a man and you brought him to your husband. I'd say that was pretty unique."

"That's not the worst of it, there's something else that's going to make Nicky even angrier with me," she told him.

"Do tell, this is most entertaining, best sport I've had in ages," encouraged Tandy.

Harriett looked at Nicky and met his eyes. There was no anger in them only gentle amusement so she took a deep breath and said, "He was starving you see, so I took him round the back of The Manor into the kitchen and I'm afraid Mrs Raynor went into hysterics. She said we were all going to be eaten alive or be poisoned if he ate off any of her plates. I cut him some bread and butter and Mrs Raynor sat holding her bosom and babbling he'd eat us all alive, stupid woman," Harriett finished.

Finally the penny dropped and Nicky asked, "You bought a negro?"

"How did you know that?" she said in surprise.

"It had something to do with Mrs Raynor saying we were all going to be eaten alive," Nicky said.

"You bought a negro? This gets better and better. Who on earth did you buy a negro from in this godforsaken place? I must say if you only paid sixpence for him you got a bargain. They can go for hundreds of pounds in the right sale." Tandy was impressed.

Harriett proceeded to tell them how she came across the crowd and how she ended up standing on the edge of town with a naked negro.

"He was naked?" asked Tandy.

"Well, he was naked except for a bit of cloth covering his modesty. He had no shoes on. I couldn't just leave him there could I?" she asked Nicky.

Tandy was in hoops of laughter and Nicky waited until he'd calmed down before he asked, "Where is this negro now?"

"I put him in the spare room next to the master bedroom. Are you very angry with me? I'm surprised the servants haven't been to see you yet to complain about the state I left Mrs Raynor in, but I'm afraid I lost all patience with her, the poor negro was scared witless."

Right on cue there was a tap on the door and Wrenshaw walked in. "Sorry to trouble you, my lord, but there is a situation in the kitchen."

"So I've been informed, Wrenshaw. I think Lady Planter is dealing with it, she is the mistress of the house now," came the reply.

"Very good, my lord." Turning to Harriett, Wrenshaw asked, "What would you have me do with Mrs Raynor, my lady?"

"Tell her to pull herself together and get on with her work or I shall have Janet replace her as cook. I know Janet does most of the cooking anyway. You can tell her to stop pretending to be ill all the time and do the job she gets paid for," Harriett told him.

"I'll pass on the message, my lady." Wrenshaw left the room.

Nicky stood up and, holding out his hand to Harriett, he said, "Let's go and take a look at your negro."

It was the most natural thing in the world for her to place her hand in his and they headed for the stairs with Tandy close on their heels.

Nicky opened the door and stood back to let Harriett go first, just in time to catch the negro sitting on the end of the bed with his sock off looking at the sole of his foot. On hearing the door open he sprung to his feet and stood upright.

"Sit down," Nicky told him. "Lift up your foot and let me have a look at it."

The negro sat down again, lifted up the sockless foot and Nicky, catching hold of his ankle, examined it. He went over to the side of the bed and pulled the bell pull.

"What's your name?" Nicky wanted to know.

"Reco," he replied.

"How long have you been in England?"

"I don't know for sure but I have seen three of your winters."

"Where do you come from?"

There was a knock on the door and Wrenshaw came in.

"Ah, Wrenshaw. I want a bowl of hot water, some soap and two clean towels," Nicky told the butler.

Giving the negro a sneaky glance, the butler closed the door behind him.

"I come from Africa."

"How did you get here?"

"I was out in the forest hunting with my ten-year-old son when I heard the sound of approaching feet. I made my son hide while I went to see who they were. We would get neighbouring tribes wandering onto our land but, to my surprise I came across these white hunters who bound me up and brought me to England in a big sailing ship. There were about a hundred and fifty of us, all crammed into the bottom of this ship; a lot didn't make it. Then we were sold, that's how I came to be in Lady Stanley's household. One day I'm going to make my way back to Africa, back to my wife and children. All I have to do is hit on a plan to make my escape, and I give you fair warning, sir, I will try my best to escape and stow away on the first ship I learn of heading for Africa."

The door opened and Wrenshaw entered with a bowl of steaming water and two towels over his arm.

"Thank you, Wrenshaw. Put the water down here." He indicated the floor in front of Reco and took the towels and soap from the servant who once more departed. Nicky bent down and felt the water; it was steaming hot. He went out and came back carrying a pitcher of cold water, poured some into the bowl and tested the water again.

"Put your feet in," Nicky told him. "I can't say I blame you, trying to escape I mean, I'd do the same."

Reco took off his other sock and placed both feet in the warm soothing water with a sign of relief. Never, since he'd been captured had Reco received such kind treatment. He had never been allowed to sit in the presence of a white man, and here he was not only being allowed to sit but, he was having his feet tended to by a gentleman of fashion. Nicky had taken one of the towels and wet it, then rubbing some soap on the towel he gently cleaned the dirt out of the badly cut soles of Reco's feet.

"How many children do you have?" asked Tandy.

"Two, a boy of ten and a six-year-old girl. They will most likely have forgotten me, they will be thirteen and nine by now," he said.

"Tandy, when did you say Captain Lally was sailing for Africa?" Nicky asked his friend.

"He'll be leaving at two o'clock in the morning, that's what he told me anyway," Tandy replied.

"How long did it take you to get here from Berkwash?"

"About four hours' steady ride."

Taking out his pocket watch, Nick said, "It's six o'clock. If you set off now you can be back there for tenish and ask Captain Lally not to weigh anchor until we get there. You know the story to tell him. Ask him if he has room for a passenger."

"Devil take it, Nicky, do you expect me to go charging back to Berkwash? I haven't had my dinner yet!" Tandy roared.

"You could go down to the kitchen and ask Mrs Raynor for something." Devilment danced in Nicky's eyes as they met his friend's.

Tandy threw a questioning glace at Harriett who told him, "I'm sure Mrs Raynor is over her shock by now and will be willing to attend to your every need."

"All I can say is you two deserve each other," he said, glancing from one to the other and adding, "I'll have to take one of your horses, mine's done in after that four-hour trek."

"You know your way to the stables. You can pick up your horse on the way back. I trust you not to break its leg."

"Break its leg, what about my neck?" asked the outraged Tandy. He took hold of Harriett's hand, brought it up to his lips and said, "Pleasure to have met you, Hetty. This is excellent sport. See you in Berkwash. 'The Whale Bone', by the way, Nick. I'll book you a room."

"In a spare room, three doors up, Harriett, you'll find a trunk packed with some old clothes of mine. Go and pack a change of clothes for Reco to take back to Africa. We can't let him go like this," Nicky said. "We don't have much time if we're to get to Berkwash before two in the morning. While you do that I'll go down to the stables and see Roy."

"I thought you might have an attic?" Harriett said, much disappointed.

"We do, I thought it would have been one of the first places you went to investigate."

"I was told I hadn't to go anywhere in the house except my room and, apart from going to the kitchen, dining room, library and this spare bedroom with Reco, I haven't been anywhere else."

"Oh for heaven's sake, woman, that was months ago when you first arrived here. I thought we'd got past all that nonsense."

"Well it's not my house. My mother taught me not to be nosey, so I am more than happy having my own room. I love it, I'm not complaining, it's bigger and better than anything I've ever had before."

"Off you go and sort some clothes out before I lose patience with you and I'll show you the attic when we get back. You have my permission to go anywhere in or on the estate as well you know, so stop being foolish. Let's get a move on. Here, Reco, finish bathing your feet. We won't be long and you'll be on your way back to Africa early in the morning with a bit of luck. Is that a good enough plan for you?"

"I can't believe this is happening to me. Are you really going to let me go back to Africa?"

"I'm sure Captain Lally will take you on board. He's a good friend of ours so Tandy will explain your position. I don't see there being a problem so long as we can get to the docks before he sails. It took Tandy four hours to get here but he was on horseback. We'll be in a wagon and it will take longer, so we will have to set off as soon as we're ready."

Holding out his hand again, he said to Harriett, "Come along, trouble, there's no time to lose."

Harriett took his hand and he led her along the passage to show her the spare bedroom. He opened the door for her, adding as she passed him, "I'm sure you'll find all you need in here."

"Thank you, I'm sure I shall," she replied.

Harriett looked round and spotted a dome-topped box and lifted up the lid. It was full of children's clothes. It wasn't until the third box was opened did she find what she was looking for. She found an old hand-held travelling bag and filled it with three shirts, three pairs of trousers, three waistcoats and three jackets. She failed to find any socks but, on opening the next wooden box she came across some old boots, so matching up three pairs of boots she added them to the travelling bag, then made her way back to the bedroom with her spoils.

"Here you are, Reco, try some of these on. You look about the same height as Nicky. Leave the rest in the travelling bag to take with you. I'll go and see if Wrenshaw knows where Nicky keeps his socks." She handed him the bag and left him to try on the clothes.

Harriett met Nicky coming back along the corridor and said, "I found some clothes and some old boots but there were no socks."

"You'll find some socks in my bedroom in the set of drawers under the window. I'll go and see how Reco is getting on," he told her as they passed each other.

Harriett went into Nicky's bedroom and found it much the same size as the one she occupied but his was much more opulent, having a large canopied four-poster bed hung with red velvet drapes. A rust-coloured carpet covered the floor. The furniture was of dark oak and the walls were covered in cream Chinese silk adorned with birds. Harriett had never seen the likes before: the colours were amazing. It was a beautiful room. She found the chest of drawers and took out six pairs of socks then made her way next door. Harriett knocked and waited to be told to go in – the last thing she wanted was to walk into the room and find Reco in a state of undress – but Nicky opened the door for her.

"I've found the socks and I have tidied up after myself," she told him.

"You should have left that for the servants to do, that's what I pay them for," he told her.

"I'm not helpless you know," she replied.

"I'm well aware of that," he responded.

Ignoring him Hetty went into the bedroom to find Reco standing in Nicky's cast-off clothes. The length was perfect but because Reco was so thin they tended to hang on him and she noted that he was wearing a belt to keep the trousers up and his feet were bare.

"Here, put these on, they'll stop the boots rubbing your feet." She handed him a pair of socks and put the rest inside the travelling bag.

When Reco was fully dressed, Nicky said, "Right, let's get going," and walked out of the room.

Reco picked up his travelling bag with all his treasures in and followed Nicky along the landing and down the stairs.

Harriett went slowly back to her room and sat on the bed, pleased that Nicky had solved the problem of Reco but also disappointed. It was her adventure and they had ridden off into the night without her.

Nicky sat patiently holding the reins waiting for Hetty to appear. When she didn't he handed Reco the reins saying, "Hold these." He jumped down and went back into the house. Seeing no sign of Hetty he ran back upstairs and into the spare bedroom, no sign of her there either. Next he went to her bedroom, knocked sharply on the door and entered to find her sitting soulfully on the edge of the bed. "What the devil are you doing?" he asked.

"Nothing," she told him.

"We're waiting for you, hurry up and finish doing your nothing, we need to be on our way," he said exasperated.

"Am I to go too?" she asked.

"Of course you are, he's your negro. Don't you want to see him off?" he wanted to know.

"Oh yes please, I'd like that above anything," she told him.

"Then come on." He held out his hand.

Harriett was getting used to this hand-holding and she had to admit to herself she liked it. They ran down the staircase together and Nicky grabbed her cloak and a couple of great coats from the cloak stand as they passed and threw them in the back of the wagon, before jumping up and taking the reins from Reco. With Harriett sitting between them they were on their way.

Clutching the seat with both hands as they set off at a pace down the drive, Harriett soon found she had no need to hang on. Nicky was a good driver and she soon relaxed into utter awe and watched the landscape rolling by. Two spare horses were tethered at the back of the wagon and Harriett asked what they were for.

"To give the lead horse a rest. We'll have to change horses at least twice before we get to Berkwash; we don't want to drive this poor horse into the ground, do we?"

"No indeed not," she said again, much impressed with his easy organized way and she lapsed into silence.

It was dark when Nicky changed the horse for the second time. Before he remounted, he reached into the back of the wagon, giving Harriett her cloak to wrap around her and handing one of the great coats to Reco. He donned the other himself before setting off again.

Glad of the extra warmth from the cloak, Harriett said, "You seem to have thought of everything, my lord."

"Having served in the Peninsular we had to think ahead. The nights are drawing in and the weather can be as unpredictable on the coast as it is on the moor. I know Captain Lally will be ready to set off. The sooner he sets sail the farther he will be away from the storms they get this time of the year out at sea. It's now or never to get Reco on his way. I suppose there'll be other ships heading for Africa but I know Captain Lally will take good care of Reco. He'll get him safely to Africa. You'll be on your own once they dock in Africa, Reco. Will you be able to find your way back to where you were taken from?"

"I'll find my way back home, have no fear on that account. I'll travel at night and hide during the day if I have to. I still can't believe you're sending me back home. This is the first kindness I've met since being captured. Am I really on my way? Look at me dressed up like a real gentleman and not only riding on the wagon but being driven by a lord. It's hard to take it all in," he told them.

Harriett's curiosity got the better of her and she asked Reco what he'd done to make the lady in the carriage want to sell him.

"She kept me locked in an ante-room next to her bedroom and, when she wanted to be made love to, she would let me out into her bedroom, and when she was finished with me I was locked back in the ante-room. I was there for three winters. Two days before she sold me, I tried to make my escape. She fell asleep before she had locked me back in the ante-room. I crept out of her bedroom to make my way outside but, not knowing the layout of the house, I walked into the library and straight into the arms of her husband. Neither of them was pleased about my attempted escape and they said they could no longer trust me. That's the reason I was sold on."

"She was married and her husband knew about you?" said a shocked Harriett.

"It was her husband who bought me for her. She said he couldn't cope with her demands and I can't say I blame him, believe me. You think I'm so thin because I've been starved of food? Well I can assure you that's not the reason."

"How is it you speak such good English?" Harriett asked.

"She taught me, Lady Stanley, she said she had nothing else to do and I was her pet. She also taught me to read, which was the only good thing about living there. I learned to read so I could read to her while she slouched on the bed. She had fallen asleep whilst I was reading to her and that's when I tried to escape. I hated her with a passion," he said with disgust.

Harriett sat in silence thinking over what he had told them and, turning to Nicky she asked, "Did you know things like this happened?"

"I've heard rumours, even of worse fates befalling the negroes that are captured and brought back to England, then sold into slavery. Not only in this country but other countries too. I think the black population is hard done by in America as well."

"Why? Why would anyone treat another human being like that?"

"Ignorance, and because they can I suppose, money can do anything if there is enough of it."

"Well, I think it's appalling," said Harriett.

"I thought you might, but you can sleep easy tonight, Hetty, knowing you have helped Reco make his escape by sending him back to his wife and children," Nicky said. "We can't change the world, Hetty, but we can make it a little bit better, if only for one unfortunate human being. See those lights up ahead, we're approaching the port of Berkwash, we'll soon be there."

All thoughts of slavery vanished from Harriett's mind. The moon was reflected on the sea and the tall ships with their huge masts were lined up, either ready to be unloaded or to set sail for distant lands. Nicky watched Harriett with delight, getting pleasure from seeing her face light up with excitement at her first sight of the sea.

Making his way along the promenade, Nicky entered the town of small closely adjacent terrace houses and found the Whale Bone Inn. He guided the horses between the archway and into a pebbled courtyard where a sleepy young stable boy came forward to take the reins.

Entering the inn, there was more than one curious or sly glance cast at the negro who was wearing a cloak with many capes. A beautiful, fresh-faced young woman glowing with life stood between him and an elegant gentleman of fashion. Harriett was looking around the inn much in awe of her surroundings. There were tables in close proximity to each other and it smelt of beer, smoke and sweat, making her turn up her nose.

A side door opened and Lord Tandleson appeared. "Ah, there you are, dear boy, glad you made it, we're in here." He indicated behind him with his head.

They followed him into the private parlour where a very tall gentleman stood up and came towards them. "It's good to see you, Nicky. I didn't think I was going to get the chance between these trips. Tandy told me you were married." He embraced Nicky and gave him an affectionate slap on the back.

"Nice to see you too, Lally. I can't thank you enough for taking Reco with you. I wouldn't trust him to anyone else, except John Grey of course, and he's on his way to Australia."

A grin spread across Captain Lally's face. "So I've been informed. You don't hang about I'll say that for you, Nicky."

"Circumstances, Lally, circumstances. Had to move before the ship sailed." His lordship grinned back.

"And this pretty little thing will be the famous Lady Planter?" Captain Lally said, holding out his hand to her.

"It is, my wife, Harriett. Harriett, this is my good friend, Captain Lally," Nicky introduced them.

"I'm very pleased to make your acquaintance, Captain Lally, but you are mistaken, I'm not famous," she told him.

"Not yet anyway, eh?" He smiled kindly down at her. "But I'm Lally to my friends and I hope we are going to be good friends, young Harriett. When I'm in dock for any length of time I descend on Nicky and stay with him until it's time to set sail again, as does Captain Grey, whom I think is having the pleasure of your fa… er… The Fat Man and his Toad on his voyage."

"Thank you, I hope we'll be friends too but I can assure you that you have the best passenger. Reco is much nicer than The Fat Man and his Toad," Harriett simply told him.

This brought a howl of laugher from the captain who replied, "Yes, Tandy told me about the whale and the eyeball. I must admit I've met a few people in my lifetime that I would like that to happen to as well."

The captain turned to Reco and held out his hand. "We have a meal ordered which will be here directly. As soon as we've eaten we must go on board ship. I have last minute checks to make, then you'll be on your way back to Africa and your family with a bit of luck."

"This is too kind of you all. I don't know what to say. Thank you doesn't seem enough for what you're all doing for me," Reco said.

"Nonsense it's the least we can do. You've been very ill treated, as have a lot of your countrymen, but there's nothing we can do for them. We'll see about getting you safely back home, have no fear," the captain told him.

The door opened and the landlord entered carrying a large white plate with a huge piece of hot steaming beef on it, and was followed by two kitchen maids with dishes of steaming vegetables. A bottle of wine was brought and the little group all sat down and served themselves, with Captain Lally carving the beef and handing it along the table.

Reco stood at the back of Harriett's chair until Nicky said, "Sit down, Reco, you're amongst friends now, and have something to eat, man."

Reco pulled out a chair and sat next to Harriett who said to nobody in particular, "This has been the most exciting thing I've ever done. I've seen the sea. I never thought I'd see the sea and I'm eating in an inn. Who would have thought it!"

"If we had the time, Harriett, I would have shown you around my ship," the captain told her.

"Would you really, I would have liked that above all things. When you're next in port I shall hold you to that. If Nicky will bring me down to the sea again, that is." She looked expectantly at her husband.

"I might think about it," he teased.

"Well if he won't, I will come and get you personally," the captain promised.

"I think you and I will get along famously Captain Lally," Harriett whispered to him.

"Better watch out, Nicky my boy. Looks like you have some competition on your hands." Tandy's eyes gleamed.

"No contest, Tandy, he's never at home," Lord Planter rallied.

"I've been thinking, Reco," said the captain. "When we get to Africa we'll hire some horses and I'll accompany you as far as the edge of your forest, just to make sure nobody tries to make you into a slave again, but once we reach the forest you'll be on your own. Can you remember how to get back to your forest?"

"I can, but you don't have to put yourself to so much trouble. I can hide during the day and travel at night. You're already doing more for me than I can ever repay," Reco told him.

"I'll reimburse you for any money you have to lay out, Lally," Nicky told him.

"You will not you know. You're a married man now and I have more money than I know what to do with. Nothing to spend it on while I'm at sea. Anyway, why should you have all the fun? I shall enjoy going on a trek and seeing some of Africa. There's a six-week wait once we arrive there before we have to return home. We have to make sure the ship is seaworthy and have any repairs carried out and all that sort of thing. So I might even venture further inland with you, we'll have to see how we go. I'm looking forward to it," Lally told them.

It was the first time Harriett had tasted wine and she had to admit to herself she would rather have had water, but she felt she had to drink it, since Captain Lally had put himself out to make things as pleasant as possible for them all. It had been a long, exciting day. She'd had an excellent meal and, once the meal was over and the landlord was clearing the dishes away, it was all she could do to keep her eyes open.

Captain Lally stood up and said, "Time marches on. I'm afraid, we must be going."

"Just a second, Lally, I have something for Reco in my bag. Have the bags been taken upstairs?" Nicky asked the landlord.

"They have, my lord. Your room is the second door on the right at the top of the stairs."

"Thank you," Nicky said as he headed for the door.

"I wonder what he's about now?" Tandy said.

The door opened and Nicky was back holding some books. "I just grabbed these, Reco, before we set off. I thought you might like to show your children where you've been." He handed Reco a book of maps. "And here are a couple of reading books, one with pictures in for your little girl. You can teach them how to read and write." He held the books out to Reco.

"Books for me, many thanks, Lord Planter. I'm sure to wake up any time now." Reco ran his fingers along the book covers.

"I'm sure Lally will show you how to read the atlas," Nicky told him.

"Sure I will but can we please go now? Say your goodbyes and I'll see you when I get back, Nicky." Again the captain embraced Nicky and headed out of the door saying, "Pleasure to have met you, Harriett. Don't forget our date."

"Never in a million years," shouted Harriett at his retreating back.

Reco hugged Harriett and whispered in her ear, "I'll never forget you, Lady Planter, ever." And he followed the captain.

"I'll go and see them off," said Tandy. "See you at breakfast."

"Well, Lady Planter, it's been a long day. I don't know about you but I'm ready for bed. I'm afraid Tandy booked us into a double room so we're going to have to share tonight, I hope you don't mind too much," Nicky said.

"Of course not. I'm nearly dropping to sleep now. I'm not used to drinking wine and I feel quite light headed," she told him.

"Let's get you to bed then, come on." He held out his hand and she placed hers in it and he led her to bed. "It's a big bed so there's plenty of room for the both of us. I would normally have slept in the armchair but I'm ready for a lie down," Nicky told her as he undressed.

Harriett tried to make her fingers undo the buttons at the front of her dress but found she had no strength in them. Nicky came around the bed and said, "Here let me do that for you." He was pleased to find she raised no objection, and he was even more pleased when he slipped her dress from her shoulders and let it fall to the ground, to see she wore nothing under her gown except a pair of white bloomers.

He held the sheets back and she climbed gratefully in, then Nicky went round to his side of the bed and finished undressing, leaving just his long drawers on and climbed in beside her. He turned to face her to find her fast asleep, but he was content to lay and watch her sleep. He couldn't resist gently lifting the blankets up and letting his eyes take their fill of her young firm breasts, and he too was soon in a blissfully peaceful sleep.

CHAPTER 7

Next morning, Harriett woke to find she was alone in bed. She swung her legs over the side and realised she was wearing nothing but her bloomers. Her face began to glow red when she recalled Lord Planter unfastening her dress and helping her into bed.

She went over to the overnight bag his lordship had brought for her and took out clean bloomers and a dress. Harriett was not used to wearing anything under her dress. She had tried on one of the bodices she'd found in the drawers in her bedroom, but it was laced at the back and she found that she could not lace it up herself, so had decided not to bother. Harriett crossed to the washstand, had a strip wash in cold water, then dressed and made her way down to the private parlour they had occupied the previous night, and found Lord Planter reading a book by the window.

"Sorry I'm late. It must have been that wine I had, I'm not used to it. I can't even remember going to sleep," she told him.

Lord Planter smiled at her and said, "At least you slept well."

"I did, but I can remember you helping me out of my dress, thank you." She blushed.

"My pleasure," he replied, holding eye contact.

Harriett felt her cheeks burning, and was nettled into saying, "I'll do the same for you some day."

"I'll look forward to it." His eyes never wavered.

Harriett turned away. Going over to the sideboard, drawn by the delicious smell of bacon and eggs, she helped herself to a plateful and tucked into it with relish. She was on her second rasher of bacon when she said to Nicky, "Aren't you having anything to eat?"

"I had mine an hour ago," he replied.

"Oh," was all she could think of to say," then adding, "Is it any good?"

"Yes, the bacon was excellent," he replied.

Harriett laughed and said, "I meant the book."

"Ah the book, it belongs to the landlady. I think you would enjoy this more than me, I'm afraid, the heroine is susceptible to fainting every other paragraph. I haven't been able to grasp the story so far but it gave me something to do to pass the time," he told her.

"Yes, I've read a couple of those books where the heroine does nothing but faint and I think it gives us females a bad name. I've never fainted in my life, except for the day we were married but that doesn't count because I wasn't very well. And nor did my mother and she had a lot to put up with I can tell you," said an indignant Harriett.

"I was in bed until eight o'clock. I think we were both tired; it had been a long day. When I came down Tandy had already departed but he left me a note. Would you like to read it?" Nicky asked her.

"If he wrote the letter to you, my lord, do you think he would mind me reading it?" she asked between mouthfuls.

"I think you made two conquests last night, Hetty, and no, Tandy won't mind if you read the letter. It mentions you," he told her. Lord Planter crossed the room and handed her the letter.

Harriett put down her knife and fork and took the offered letter and read:

> To: Lord Planter
> Nick, my boy, still abed I see, well can't blame you.
> Dashed pretty girl you've got there and lively too.
> Reco got on his way all right, no hold ups. I decided to set off home before you pack me off to India or some such place. You're not safe to be around.
> Lally sends his love to Hetty, as do I. See you both soon.
> Yours,
> Tandy.

"What does he mean 'you're not safe to be around'?" Harriett asked.

"I think he's referring to my sending The Fat Man to Australia and Reco off to Africa." Nicky smiled.

Harriett thought this was very amusing and Nicky joined in her amusement. "I like your friends," she told him.

"Good, I'm pleased to hear it. We've all been friends a long time and it seems they've taken a liking to you too. I'm going to have to keep an eye on them I can see," he teased. "If you've finished your breakfast I'm afraid we must be on our way. The weather is going to change and we have a long drive in front of us, and we're in an open wagon. I was going to spend another night here and show you the sights, but we'll be coming back to let Lally show off his ship."

"Did he mean it, about showing me round his ship? I thought he was just teasing me."

"He'll be back to show you round; there's nothing he likes better than showing off," Nicky told her.

"I'll just run upstairs to use the chamber pot before we set off." Harriett jumped up and headed for the stairs.

The sky was overcast as they set off at a fast trot with Nicky making expert manoeuvres, passing pedestrians and other horse-drawn carriages which were coming in the opposite direction.

"Don't worry, I won't overturn us," Nicky told her.

"I'm not worried, you seem to be a crack hand with the reins," she replied.

A comfortable silence fell between them as the outskirts of the port town was reached and the desolate moor began to appear. Harriett looked around her: the scene was dull and grey with dark clouds amassing overhead. She had seen such weather many times and was used to the quiet isolation, but more than anything she felt safe, safer than she had ever done in her life.

Her trust in Lord Planter was something she was still getting used to. Harriett had never trusted The Fat Man or his Toad, nor had she felt as safe as this, even when her mother had been alive. There had always been the threat of The Fat Man hanging over her but Lord Planter had taken that threat away.

The Fat Man was on his way to the other side of the world, but even if he wasn't Harriett knew she would be safe under Lord Planter's protection. She need never be afraid of The Fat

Man or his Toad again; they were gone. Not only had he taken away that threat but he had done it without complaint and with an ease she was unaccustomed to. He had never given her a telling off, not once, not even when she'd told him off about Jenny or when she'd brought a negro home. If it had been Jimmy, she would never have heard the last of it. How many times had he told her she had to stop getting herself into these scrapes? He had made hard work of everything she had ever dragged him into.

Lord Planter said, "Now we're out of the main traffic there's something I have to tell you. You remember Jenny from the milliner's shop? Well I went to see Madam Grace and I bought Jenny from her, but things didn't go as I had expected. Jenny was terrified. She wouldn't get out of the coach, she was cowering on the floor covering her face with her hands and crying. I tried to pick her up to bring her into The Manor but she started kicking and screaming fit to wake the dead. She just wouldn't get out of the carriage even for Sally. You weren't around so I decided to take her to the convent. I've known the nuns nearly all my life. My mother used to take me when I was a boy. She donated money to them and I have carried on the tradition. She will be well cared for and they will help her get over whatever it is that's wrong with her. Mother Mary Joan is in charge of her and she's going to write to me when there's improvement. I still haven't heard from her, so I thought we might have a drive over to see how she's getting on, if the weather permits that is, and it's all right with you."

Harriett looked at him and asked, "Are you a mind reader?"

"Not as far as I know. You never cease to amaze me, Hetty. Having told you about Jenny, I never expected that remark from you," he said.

"I was just thinking about Jenny. I never expected you to come out with what you've just told me. You've never mentioned this before," she accused him.

"She was in a state, Hetty. I didn't want to upset you, it's a good job you didn't see her. What on earth had that woman said to her to frighten the poor child like that? I was waiting to hear from the convent, hoping there was good news so I could take you over and see her but, as I just said, I'm still waiting to hear from them. I'm going to have to change the horse now. We have about another hour and a half of driving to do before we get to the next inn, where we'll stop for something to eat. Then with another change of horse, we should be back home by six o'clock. So far we've been lucky and the rain has held off. Let's see how far we can get before the sky opens."

Lord Planter jumped down and went to the rear of the wagon to untie one of the spare horses and Harriett thought about Jenny. All this time she hadn't given Jenny a thought. There had been so much going on in her life since she came to The Manor that Jenny had been forgotten. Lord Planter had been to see her and removed her from Madam Grace and taken her to a convent. A convent would be the ideal place for Jenny. It was quiet, secluded with no men.

How kind he was. He was so different from what she thought he would be like when she first came to live with him. Harriett couldn't bear to think about not having him in her life now. But she had spoilt his life. He was married to someone way below his station. He had never entered her bedroom to demand his marital rights, something she had been dreading when she first arrived, but now the thought of him thinking so badly of her made her heart sink.

Last night they had shared the same bed at the inn. Not that she remembered much about that, all she could remember was watching him undress and seeing his powerful naked back as he sat on the edge of the bed, bent over taking off his boots. The thought made her stomach turn over and her heart begin to beat a little faster.

Lord Planter, having finished changing the horse, climbed back on board, took up the reins and set off again. After they had travelled for half an hour in silence, Nicky turned to give her a quick glance and his heart sank. "Are you angry with me for taking Jenny to the convent without telling you?" he asked.

"How could I be angry with you for being so kind? It's the ideal place for Jenny. I know she was disturbed, by the things she would say to me about what animals men were, and she hoped she'd never have to see one and that she hoped she could live with Madam Grace all her life. I tried to tell her that all men aren't the same but she wouldn't listen to me. Of course I'm not angry with you," she added quietly.

"After your experience with men I wonder you don't feel the same about us," he told her.

"My mother told me about the life she had before The Fat Man. She told me about my grandfather and grandmother, and about the balls and the beautiful gowns and elegantly dressed gentlemen. Some nice and some not so nice but she also told me the same about women; some were nice and some not so nice. Jimmy was my friend, my only friend and he's one of the nice ones. He'd do anything for me, even if he did moan and complain all the time. Not like you. You haven't shouted at me once for the scrapes I've been in."

"Nothing to shout about, Hetty. I agree with you about good and bad in both sexes. I've met some not so nice women in my life and some not so nice men too. Mr Meanwood, for example, he certainly took me in. If I'd taken more interest in what was going on at The Manor, he wouldn't have got away with what he did. When you brought Reco to The Manor and you had a run in with Mrs Raynor, it wasn't until you mentioned that Janet did most of the cooking anyway, that I looked into it and found you were right. Mrs Raynor did tend to sneak off to her bed and leave Janet to do the work. You handled that situation very well by the way, I was impressed." He shot her a sideways glance.

"I thought you'd be angry with me for upsetting your cook," she admitted.

"Well you thought wrong. Sometimes you have to deal with a situation that makes you unpopular, but it still has to be done. Here we are. Time for something to eat. I don't know about you but I'm starving. Last port of call before we reach home." He pulled up at the front of a wayside inn and, jumping down, he made his way round to Harriett's side and held up his hands to help her down. He held her close for a few seconds feeling her young soft body next to his. A young boy ran to take the reins and the moment was lost.

"Have the grey horse hitched up to the wagon while we eat and there's a shilling in it for you," his lordship told the young boy.

"Yes, sir, thank you, sir, and I'll give them something to eat and drink as well for a shilling." The young boy grinned.

After a satisfying meal, Harriett climbed back onto the wagon with the grey horse now at the head and the young boy happily biting the silver coin Lord Planter had tossed to him. They set off with the sky looking heavy with rain.

"I don't think the rain will hold off much longer," Lord Planter said, and no sooner had the words left his lips than they felt the first drops of rain.

"Hold the reins, Hetty. Just keep to this steady trot and you'll be all right. The horse is well behaved." He handed her the reins.

Harriett took hold of the reins as Lord Planter placed his arm around her and showed her how to hold them correctly between her fingers. Once she had the feel of it he slowly took his arm from around her and, keeping a watchful eye, turned to reach into the back box in the wagon. He took out a large waterproof tarpaulin and placed it over both their heads and shoulders.

"This won't stop us getting wet, Hetty, but at least it will stop the rain running down the back of our neck," he told her.

"Is this another tip you picked up from your time in the Peninsular?" she asked.

He smiled at her and said, "It could be."

"What was it like out there?" she wanted to know.

"Not very nice. I didn't enjoy the fighting. I was glad to get back home," he admitted.

They trotted along with Harriet holding the reins and Lord Planter with his arm across her shoulders holding the tarpaulin in place. "Do you want to take over the reins?" she asked him.

"No, you're doing fine. I'm going to teach you to drive, then you can take the gig out anytime you like. I don't like you wandering around the moor on foot," he told her.

"I've always walked the moor. I grew up on the moor, I love the wildness of it and the beauty," she countered.

"That's as maybe but you are now my wife and I have to think of your safety. You will be safer if you have a gig under you," he insisted.

"I don't see how you work that out. What if I hit a pothole and overturn it and it lands on top of me? I could be laid there days before anyone found me," she said.

"If you didn't return home I'd send out a search party for you but that is not what I meant about your safety. We are very wealthy, Hetty, and people like The Fat Man, think of ways of relieving us of it. It has been known for husbands or wives to be taken and held for ransom. I don't want to frighten you but you must be aware that there are some very nasty types out there. Look how easy it was for The Fat Man to gain entry onto our land and grab hold of you. You've lived a very sheltered life, Hetty. Things are very different living in society. I need you to be watchful, to look out for yourself and to be aware that there are predators of the human kind. You have such an innocent and trusting nature, Hetty. I don't want anything to happen to you. You know what The Fat Man is like. There are much worse types than him knocking about, much more violent as well. Do you understand what I am saying?" he asked.

She didn't reply for a few minutes while she considered what he'd said. "Yes, Nicky, I understand what you are saying. You're right, I never thought about it like that. Look what happened to my mother. She was on her way to church when The Fat Man struck and yes, I was taken by surprise in the woods when The Fat Man grabbed me. Thank you for pointing it out to me, I shall be much more vigilant and aware from now on."

"Good, I will also teach you to shoot and provide you with a small hand pistol that you can keep in your purse or pocket," he added. "We are nearly home, see how easy it is to drive the wagon? You'll soon be seen flying around the town on your own little gig.

"What about Roy teaching me to bare-knuckle fight?" she asked.

"That is taking things a bit too far I think," he replied.

They were approaching the closed gates of The Manor and Nicky told her to gently pull back on the reins and the horse came to a standstill. He jumped down and opened the gates and took the horse's head and led it through the gates before going to close them again. He jumped back beside Harriett and told her to give the reins a little flick and the horses started to walk slowly up the drive.

After dinner that evening Lord Planter said to Harriett, "Let's go into the drawing room. I have something to show you." He stood up and took hold of Harriett's chair and pulled it away from the table for her.

Once settled Lord Planter said, "I have had a letter from the convent, I think you should read it."

He took the letter from inside his jacket and handed it to her and she read:

Dear Lord Planter,

Sorry I haven't written to you before now but there hasn't been much to relate to you. As you so rightly said Jenny is a very disturbed child and we could not get her to even venture out of her room.

Three weeks ago a gentleman came to see us bringing his granddaughter with him, she too was much disturbed but she was exactly the opposite of Jenny. She had been badly treated by her mother who had poured boiling water over her hand when she had broken a cup. This is only one of the incidents that had befallen this poor child and it was only by the grace of God that her grandfather had that day called to see them. He saw the state of the child's hand. He had insisted on Jane telling him what had happened. He then learnt of other ill treatment suffered at the hands of her mother so he took her away and brought her here.

We decided to put the two girls in a room together and it would seem they are becoming good friends.

There are also signs, from both girls that to some extent, their shared trauma is helping them. They both seem to be starting to live a little. Jenny is now venturing outside for a few hours and they have started reading classes and are enjoying it.

I would ask you, however, not to come and see her for another two months or so as the least little thing might undo all the good work that the nuns have been doing with them.

I don't have any objection to letters, however. Jane receives letters from her grandfather and she enjoys getting them so if you feel inclined to write to Jenny, hopefully, she will look forward to receiving them. I have written to Jane's grandfather telling him the same. I will write to you again in a few weeks to let you know of any further progress.

Yours faithfully,
Mother Mary Joan

Harriett looked up at Lord Planter who stood with his elbow resting on the mantelpiece watching her read. "This sounds good news. Is it all right if I write to her?" she asked.

"Of course, I'm sure she would rather hear from you than me." He smiled.

The next two weeks dragged for Harriett, the rains had come and she was forced to spend most of the time reading in her room. She had also written a long letter to Jenny.

Harriett came to the end of her novel and closed the book. She was bored. She walked over to the window and looked out over the wet lawn towards the wood. She hadn't even been down to see Jimmy. What a lot she had to tell him. So much had happened to her in the past two weeks and she couldn't wait to go and tell him.

CHAPTER 8

Next morning Harriett woke and, going over to the window, she drew back the curtains. It was still early and she was restless, tired of stopping in and to her delight the sun was just beginning to rise and the rain had stopped.

She got washed and dressed and putting on a strong pair of boots she set out, intending to go and see Jimmy, but it was so early she decided to go the long way round. Harriett cut through the woods, heading towards the river. Her intention was to walk along the riverbank, cutting back across the field and back through the wood to the home farm.

It was heavy going; under foot the grass was saturated and soggy. This didn't deter Harriett: she was pleased to be outside in the fresh air. It was a bit easier going through the wood but once she was out of the wood and onto the riverbank her feet began to sink into the sodden grass again.

The sound of the swollen river rushing by was deafening, and the water nearly reached to the top of the riverbank. She followed the flow to the bend where the river made a sharp turn to the right and there, in the elbow of the swollen river, debris and flotsam had collected and a large tree trunk was held fast.

At first Harriett thought it was another piece of wood on top of the tree, but as she got closer she realized it was the body of a man lying full length across it. She shouted to him at the top of her voice but the sound of the rushing river drowned it out. There was nothing she could do so she lifted up her skirt and ran back to The Manor.

Lord Planter had also risen early and he was sitting at his desk when he heard the front door open with a bang and Harriett shouting, "Nicky, Nicky, Nicky."

He jumped up and opened the library door to see Harriett with her dress covered in mud and her cheeks bright red with cold and exercise. "What the devil's the matter?" he demanded.

Harriett ran up to him and grabbed his lapels. "Nicky, come quickly, there's a man, in the river, and I couldn't reach him."

"Where in the river?" he asked.

"You know where the river bends, all kinds of rubbish have been washed down and there's a huge tree caught in it with a man on top of it. I shouted to him but the noise of the river is so loud he couldn't hear me, or he's dead," she panted.

"Go get some blankets and meet me out front," he told her as he turned away.

"Blankets!" she said. "There's no time for blankets, we have to get to him straight away."

He turned and came back to her and took her face in his hands and asked, "How are we to get him home once we've got him out of the river, Hetty? I'm going to hitch up the wagon while you go and get some blankets. He'll need to be kept as warm as we can make him until we can get him home."

Realising he was right she said, "Yes, you're right, sorry."

He couldn't resist bending down and kissing her lightly on the lips and adding, "Good girl."

Lord Planter headed for the stables and Harriett flew up the stairs her face pink from embarrassment, but still feeling the pleasant pressure of his lips fleetingly brushing hers. She went to the linen box in her bedroom and took out an armful of blankets hoping there would be enough, then, running back downstairs she waited impatiently on the porch, until finally, Lord Planter come slowly round the side of The Manor and pulled up beside her.

Throwing the blankets in the back of the wagon, she climbed up beside him and said, "You were an age, I thought you were never coming."

"I've had to hitch up the wagon myself. Roy and Tim went to Trembleton yesterday to buy feed for the horses and they had to stay over for the night so there's nobody at the stables. I also had to find some ropes and a life jacket. I came as quickly as I could. We'll have to do this between us, there's no time to go looking for help. I've left instructions for a fire to be lit in the blue bedroom and some bed warmers to be placed in the bed for when we get back," he told her.

"He's in a very funny spot, Nicky. I don't know how we can possibly reach him. I think he's dead." She looked up at him for reassurance.

"Until we find out for sure, let's believe him to be alive and do the best we can once we get there, there's nothing else we can do, Hetty."

"I know. Can't you go any faster?" she asked.

"No I can't. The ground is saturated and I don't want the horse breaking a leg, it will not help the situation. I'm going as fast as I dare."

"I'm sorry, I don't mean to complain but I had such a fright when I saw the body lying on top of the log and there was nothing I could do. I felt so helpless."

"Don't worry we'll get him out one way or another," he told her.

As they neared the river further up to where Harriett had come out of the wood, the noise of the rushing water could be heard, and Lord Planter's heart sank when he saw the extent to which the water had risen and saw how fast it was flowing.

Approaching the bend Lord Planter spotted the figure lying prone along the log and he shouted to Harriett, "You were right, Hetty, he is in a very difficult spot." He drew the horse to a standstill and jumped down to take stock of the situation.

"I'm going to turn the wagon round, Hetty, so the back of the wagon is facing the river, and then I'm going to put one of the ropes along the ground across the back wheels to stop it from sliding backwards. Then I'll fasten the other ropes to the wagon and I want you to go to the head of the horse. I have to go into the river to be able to reach the young man, so when I raise my arm I want you to gently lead the horse forward so it can drag us both out. Do you think you can do that?"

"No, I'll go into the river, Nicky. I'm lighter than you and I know you wouldn't let me drown," she shouted back.

Then she started unbuttoning her dress and Nicky shouted back at her, "What are you doing?"

"I can't swim with all these clothes on, they'll drag me down," she shouted back, dropping the gown onto the floor then picking it up and throwing it into the wagon.

"I can't let you do this, Hetty. It's too dangerous."

"Not as dangerous as you going in and expecting me to drag you out. It's all right I can swim you know." She pulled off her boots and bloomers and stood in front of him naked.

Knowing it was pointless to argue with her and being aware that time was precious, he tied one of the ropes round her waist, then he made her hold up her arms and he placed the lifebelt over them and shouted at her, "Go in further upstream, then I can stop you from crashing into the log as the force of the water takes you. Ideally you should be going in downstream, but there's nowhere for you to enter the water with all the debris that's collected on the bend. When you reach him I will throw you a couple of ropes with a loop at the end. See if you can pull the loops over each arm, then try to roll him gently into the water. Did you hear what I said?"

Harriett nodded and sitting down on the bank she slid into the rushing water. The lifebelt kept her afloat and the dragging of the rope round her waist stopped her from being washed away, but the intense cold took her breath away. Instinct made her start to kick her legs and she glided towards the log. She hit the log harder then she expected and she felt it move, keeping still until the log settled. She looked over at Nicky and he threw her the first rope. She was having difficulty using her arms because of the lifebelt, so she pulled herself onto the log, took off the lifebelt and, pulling the man's arms up over his head, she pushed the lifebelt down along his arms until she reached his head. She eased herself nearer to the lifeless body and lifted up his head, pushing the lifebelt down as far as she could.

Taking the rope Nicky had thrown her, she placed it over his hand and up along his arm until it reached his armpit. Harriett was so cold she could hardly feel her fingers. She was

110

shivering from head to foot and it had taken her longer than she would have liked to get the first rope up his arm. She turned and held up her hand and Nicky threw her the second rope and she repeated the procedure.

Taking a deep breath, she slid off the log and she felt the tension tighten as Nicky pulled on the rope round her waist. Harriett took hold of the young man's arm furthest away from her and pulled him slowly over onto his back and into the water. The lifebelt kept him afloat but his head went backwards and she just caught it in time to stop it going under the water.

Nicky pulled on the ropes and slowly they reached the bank with Harriett kicking her legs for all she was worth, but she was beginning to have no feeling in her legs. She felt her hip bang into the side of the riverbank and the lifebelt got stuck in the mud. Placing her feet on the slimy riverbank side, she pulled the lifebelt clear and Nicky was able to drag both of them out of the water and onto dry land.

As soon as they were safely away from the water's edge, Nicky came over to Harriett and helping her stand up. He took off the rope and wrapped one of the blankets round her. "Dry off and get dressed while I get these wet clothes off this young man." He turned and started ripping off the wet clothes.

Harriett rubbed herself down quickly, scrambled into her bloomers and dress, then dried her feet and put on her boots. "What do you want me to do?" she shouted, looking up.

Movement in the river caught her eye and she stood rooted to the spot. "Nick, look!" She pointed back up along the raging river.

Being swept downstream at great speed was another tree that had been uprooted by the force of the water. They watched in silence as the tree approached the bend. They thought it was going to pass the tree that the young man had been lying across, but a rogue root clipped it and the tree slowly moved out with the current. It too headed down stream dragging all the debris with it in its wake.

"I want you to damn well do as you're told. Next time I put a lifebelt on you, leave it on and don't take it off until I give you permission, that's what I want you to do," he roared answering her previous question.

"I had to take it off. I couldn't work with it on. Anyway I knew you had me safe, I wasn't frightened."

"Well I was, don't you ever do that again."

"Don't worry I won't, it was freezing in that water. Next time I see someone floating down stream, I'll let them get on with it."

Nicky had to laugh at her and he said, "Oh for heaven's sake, take off his boots."

It was with some difficulty that the boots and clothes were discarded and the young man laid naked on the grass.

"Now, Harriett, take hold of his feet and let's get him into the wagon. Lay him on this blanket and let's wrap it round him."

Lord Planter was laying out one of the blankets as he spoke, then, taking hold of the young man under his arms while Harriett took his feet, the limp body was laid on the blanket which they then wrapped round him. Nicky took the other blankets and placed them one at a time over the top of the young man, while ever practical Harriett, bundled up his wet clothes and placed them on a ledge between the axle and the wagon.

"Come on, Hetty, hurry up. We need to get him back as quickly as possible. He's like a block of ice," Nicky shouted.

"I know he's like a block of ice, so am I," complained Harriett as she scrambled back onto the wagon.

"That was a very silly and irresponsible thing to do while you were in the river. I didn't put the lifebelt on you for the good of my health, it was there to help keep you afloat," Nicky scolded her.

"It's all right for you to sit there telling me it was for my own good. I couldn't work with it on. It restricted my arms and anyway it was better for him to have it on than me. I told you I could swim," she replied.

"You can swim in normal circumstances, Hetty, but they weren't normal. The water flow was rapid and the current very strong. It would have been easy to get washed away, you wouldn't have stood a chance," he said.

"I knew you had me safe, Nicky. I was freezing though, I could hardly feel my fingers and my legs were beginning to go numb. I don't think I could have stayed in much longer, but all's well, we've got the young man out. Do you think he's still alive?" she asked.

"I don't know, it was hard to tell, he was so cold. The good thing was he wasn't stiff. Let's hope he's just suffering from the cold, and when we get some warmth back into his body he'll be all right. We don't know how long he's been in that cold water, but at least he must have been alive when he climbed onto that log so I don't think he will have drowned."

They were approaching The Manor and Harriett could see two of the male servants waiting on the porch, and as Lord Planter drew to a halt, they went round to the back of the wagon. Taking hold of the inert figure, they lifted him down from the back of the wagon and took him upstairs to the blue room.

Harriett and Lord Planter followed. There was a blazing fire roaring up the chimney and Harriett could see several bed-warmer handles sticking out from under the bedclothes.

"Go and get changed, Hetty. Get into something warm and dry while we get this young man into bed." Nicky held the door open for her. She turned and headed for her own bedroom without a word.

CHAPTER 9

Whilst Harriett had been busy saving the young man, Jimmy was up on the roof of the empty cottage next to his. He had renovated all the cottages belonging to the home farm and a feeling of satisfaction came over him. He had transformed the cottages from near dereliction to smart habitable dwellings. Then a feeling of desperation came over him. After he'd finished repairing this last cottage, there was nothing left for him to do. This had been the best time of his life. None of the other farmhands had called him names; they had become his friends. He'd put on weight and all the fresh air and sunshine had given him a nice tan. He had become a very handsome young man although he didn't know it.

He saw Sarah Brown walking between the cottages with a basket over her arm heading towards his cottage, and his heart began to beat a little faster as he followed her progress. Sarah was not much over five feet but her plump little body aroused feelings he didn't know he possessed. He felt even more desperate than ever. He'd nothing to offer any woman. How could he even think about Sarah? He had no home, no job or prospects, no money and to top it off, he was a cripple, poor as a church mouse. What would she want with him? She could do much better for herself.

Sarah was the seventeen-year-old daughter of Mr and Mrs Brown. Mrs Brown had taken to baking Jimmy a loaf of bread when she baked for them and Sarah always insisted on delivering it. She had her eye on Jimmy, but she was finding it harder than she expected to get him interested in her. She didn't have this much trouble with the boys from the village.

Seeing Jimmy on the roof of the cottage, Sarah shouted up to him, "My mother has sent you some bread," and holding up the basket she sent him a dazzling smile, which nearly brought him down to earth with a bang.

"Thank your mother for me, will you? Just leave it on the kitchen table. I want to get this done before the rain starts again," he shouted down.

Sarah walked into Jimmy's cottage and slapped the bread down on the table and turned to leave. But the smell of new baked bread brought the flies, so she scooped up the bread and put it in his larder. She turned and walked out wondering why she bothered; she didn't look up to say goodbye on leaving his cottage.

He watched her walk away with a heavy heart and a longing so deep it hurt. He had never felt sorry for himself in all the years he'd had to stand up for himself, through all the name calling and hard times. But now he'd had this taste of happiness, he didn't think he could bear to go back to the loneliness that had followed him through his short life. He bent his head and carried on thatching the cottage roof.

Sarah went back home, stormed into the cottage, threw the basket on the table and burst into tears.

"Whatever's the matter with you?" asked her mother.

"It's Jimmy. I've tried everything I know to get him interested in me and he's never so much as tried to hold my hand. He's up on the roof of that cottage next to his and he didn't even come down to speak to me. All he said was to thank me for the bread," she sobbed.

"Don't take on so, Sarah. Some men need more pushing than others. I'm sure he'll come round, and if not, there are plenty of others from the village chasing your skirt," said her mother.

"I don't want any of the others from the village, I want Jimmy. Don't you dare make him any more bread. He doesn't deserve it. Let him make his own bread. If he's not interested in me then he won't get any more bread," she told her mother.

"That seems a bit harsh, to cut off his bread just because he's not falling all over you like the boys from the village." Her mother smiled.

"It's not funny," she shouted at her mother and ran out of the cottage crying.

Mr Brown had been sitting smoking his pipe in front of the fire and he turned to look at his wife and she laughed. "You'd better go and have a word with that young man, Ted, or he might end up starving to death."

"Not me, I'm not getting mixed up in that sort of thing, they'll have to sort it out between them. Good God, Phyllis, he must be twenty-four at least. I'm not going to go and tell him about the birds and bees. He should know by now, and if he doesn't he'll have to learn like the rest of us," Ted replied.

"He's had such a hard life, Ted. I think he thinks he's not good enough for her because of his limp. He's no idiot. He's seen the boys from the village hanging around her. All he needs is a little push in the right direction," Phyllis said.

"Then you go and do the pushing," dug in her husband.

"This is a man thing, Ted, go and see him **NOW** or there'll be no bread for you either until this is sorted one way or another. We'll never have a moment's peace and quiet if you don't," threatened Phyllis.

"Kids, we never seem to do anything but sort out the kids. Whose idea was it to have four of them? If it's not one it's the other." Ted made no effort to move but sat puffing on his pipe.

"If you hadn't been so keen to get me into bed, Ted Brown, there wouldn't have been four of them. You've nobody to blame but yourself. If you think about it, Jimmy could take one of them off your hands." Phyllis looked innocently at her husband.

"Put it like that I might have a walk by his cottage. You're a shrewd woman." Ted gave her a playful slap on the bottom as he passed.

Ted found Jimmy in the barn searching through the now depleted rubble. "Lost something?" he asked.

"Mr Brown, sorry I didn't hear you come in, you made me jump." Jimmy smiled.

"Well, lad, I've been sent on an errand of mercy," Ted told him.

"Errand of mercy, is someone wanting help?" Jimmy asked.

"Yes they are, and that someone is me," said Ted.

"Anything I can do to help, you've only to ask," he replied.

"Good, in that case you can marry that lass of mine and put us all out of our misery or we'll all starve to death," Ted said.

Jimmy felt his face go red. "I can assure you, sir, there's nothing I would like more than to marry Sarah, but my circumstances are too uncertain for me to ask a young lady, especially one as pretty as Sarah, to be my wife. Anyone in his right mind would jump at the chance of marrying her, she's beautiful."

"Have you told her that?"

"Of course not, how can I? Anyway all the lads in the village are after her. What would she want with a cripple?"

"Why do you keep calling yourself a cripple, Jimmy? You have a limp, which hardly makes you a cripple. Have you seen yourself lately, now you've filled out a bit and had some fresh air and sunshine? You're a very good looking young man and I'm afraid our Sarah has her heart set on you, so until she's caught you there'll be no peace at our house. I daren't go home until we have come to an understanding one way or another. Phyllis is on the warpath and she can be mighty persuasive, let me tell you. Is having a limp the only reason you don't want our Sarah? Because if you are dead set against her, then I will tell her so. It's no good keeping her hanging on."

"Dead set against her! Look, Mr Brown, I came here to do a bit of repair work on the cottages and I found a home and people I like. I've had the best time of my life living here. These past six months have been a touch of paradise but I know it can't last. You've all been so good to me and Mrs Brown bakes the best bread in the world. I'll have to leave soon. I've done all I can to the cottages. There's only the empty one left to finish off inside, then there's no more work for me here. How can I ask Sarah to leave this wonderful place where she's safe and loved, to follow me back to living in a cellar with hardly anything to eat and only the clothes on her back?"

Jimmy took a deep breath and continued, "Believe me, Mr Brown, I couldn't ask her to do that. You've no idea how I've had to survive. I've no idea how I have survived, and that's living on my own. How can I provide for a wife and children?

No, she's better off here under your protection. I wouldn't ask her to even think about coming with me. I've had some hard times."

"We've all had some hard times, Jimmy. I have a wife and four kids to feed. Until Lady Planter came and things changed around here, all the workers on the home farm were under threat of losing their livelihood. We had no way of telling what was to become of us, but I'll tell you this, Jimmy, no matter what happens I would always want Phyllis by my side, and if anything happened to any of our children I don't think we could bear it." Mr Brown paused.

"Looking into the future is no excuse for taking what happiness you can in the present. If you get the chance to have a crack at it, grab it with both hands. Even if you have only a fleeting glimpse of happiness in this uncertain world, it's worth savouring. Would you have missed coming here Jimmy? Your future was uncertain when you came but you came anyway, and look what happened, a little bit of paradise, if only for six months. Would you rather have missed it and never experienced it, even if you do end up back in that cellar?"

"No, I wouldn't have missed if for the world, but there was only me. I don't want to take Sarah away from all this to live in misery with me, I'd never forgive myself."

"It seems to me that you're a very selfish young man Jimmy. I wouldn't have thought so, but all through this conversation it's been all about you. What about Sarah? A marriage is for two people not one. If decisions are made between a couple then both should have a say in the matter. How do you know that Sarah would be happier living with someone she hates, who has loads of money, rather than making a living alongside the person she loves? I think you do my Sarah an injustice, Jimmy."

"I can assure you I don't. What would Sarah want with a cripple when she can have anyone she wants?"

"I think we've covered this ground before, Jimmy. Why do you keep insisting you're a cripple? I don't think anybody here on the farm classes you as anything but a very talented handyman. Your carpentry is exceptional and your willingness to lend a hand where it's needed has not gone unnoticed. You've made friends here because you are a very nice young man and I'd be proud to call you my son-in-law. You're one of us, not some sad scrounging good-for-nothing layabout. Have some self-respect, Jimmy. Mrs Brown thinks you're the right person for our Sarah and I must admit I find your company more than amenable. If you were to ask for my daughter's hand I'd have no objection. She went off in a paddy somewhere crying her eyes out. You'd better go and find her and bring her home. Just one thing, women are funny creatures. Don't tell Sarah about our conversation or she'll think I made you go and see her, then she'll have nothing to do with either of us for a couple of weeks. Never can fathom them out. They get what they want, then they don't want it, best to keep it under your hat." He gave Jimmy a wave and headed back home.

Jimmy took some time to reason with himself. He'd put all his difficulties that lay ahead of him on the table to Sarah's father and he still wanted him for a son-in-law, and thinking about it, since he'd come to live at The Manor he'd hardly thought about his limp or his future; he was content.

Then there was Sarah. He'd had more than one uncomfortable thought about her since she'd taken to calling most days with a loaf of bread or the odd eggs or rasher of bacon. She'd stop and talk to him, even sitting down on his doorstep while he worked on his own cottage of an evening. He'd grown used to her visits and anticipated her arrival with more pleasure than was good for him. What if he never saw her again? What if he had to leave this little bit of paradise? Mr Brown was right he had to take what happiness he could, while he could.

Jimmy threw his hammer down, wiped his hands down his trousers and went in search of Sarah.

While working up on the rooftops, he'd watched Sarah many a time walk across the field to a little secluded patch with a fallen tree at the edge of the wood, where she'd sit in the sunshine and mend torn clothes, or just sunbathe and no doubt dream of romance or of a knight in shining armour galloping towards her and transporting her off to his castle in the sky. Well he was no knight in shining armour and he certainly didn't possess a castle, but he intended to offer her what he had, which was very little.

Jimmy found her sitting on her fallen tree blowing her nose. "You'll end up with a red nose if you carry on blowing it like that," he said.

She spun round at the sound of his voice and sobbed, "What do you care?"

"Not a jot, it's not my nose."

"Go away."

"Why are you crying?"

"It's none of your business."

"I might be able to help."

"Well you can't."

"You could try me."

"There, I've stopped crying now so go away."

122

"Has one of the boys from the village upset you?"

"No."

Have you had a row with your mother or father?"

"No."

"May I sit down?"

"No."

He sat down anyway. "I came to see if you have any objections to my asking your father if he would mind if I paid court to you."

She was too stunned to speak; she just looked up at him with her mouth slightly open.

He put a finger under her chin and said, "The flies will get in," gently pushing her mouth shut. "I have to tell you though, I don't have much to offer you. In fact I don't have anything to offer you. I might be out of work any day now I've nearly finished the cottages and I have no idea what will happen next. All I have to offer you is my heart, Sarah. It's not much I know, but it's all yours if you want it. We certainly can't live on it, so I want you to think very carefully about it before you decide if you want me for your beau. I can't expect you to leave the comfort of your home to come and live on the road with me, looking for work with no roof over your head. It's no life, Sarah. I know, I've lived it. If things were different I'd kidnap you and run off with you so none of the boys from the village can get you. I've seen them all chasing you, but I love you. I just wanted you to know that, just in case I have to leave."

"I love you too."

"Come here." He held out his arms and she melted into them.

"I don't care if you have a job or not, we can work things out together. We've had hard times too you know. My mother has

123

had to take washing in to help feed us all. I can work. I'm not afraid of what the future has in store. All I know is that you have become the centre of my life and I couldn't bear it if you went away. Please promise me you'll never leave me, Jimmy."

"I promise, I will do everything in my power to provide a living for us," he replied.

"Can we go and tell my mother?" she asked him.

"If you want to, but don't forget, if we want to get married I will have to ask Lord Planter's permission and hope that he agrees to it."

CHAPTER 10

Harriett went into her bedroom and found there was a blazing fire going in the grate. She went over to it and held out her hands rubbing them together. Going to the wardrobe, she took out a thick woollen gown, some clean bloomers and a pair of thick woollen socks. She stripped off the damp clothes and stood naked in front of the fire letting the heat penetrate her cold body. Her feet were the worst; she could hardly feel them. Taking hold of the mantelpiece with one hand for balance, she stood on one foot and held the other to the fire wriggling her toes.

At that moment the door opened and Lord Planter walked in. Harriett's face went bright red and it had nothing to do with the heat from the fire.

"I've come to see if you're all right. I saw you crash into the side of the riverbank." His eyes passed over her body.

"I'm fine, thank you, just a bit cold that's all."

"Even if you weren't you wouldn't admit to it, let me see your side."

Harriett had forgotten about that but she was so cold she couldn't feel anything. She turned sideways and tried to see for herself. There was a dark graze running down the side of her hip.

"It must be nothing, I can't feel it."

"Not now you can't but I'm betting by the morning a dirty big bruise will be there as well. It needs cleaning. Stay where you are by the fire."

He went over to the washstand and, taking the soft towel, he dipped it in the water and came back to the fire and gently cleaned the wound. "I'll get the doctor to have a look at it when he arrives. He's been sent for, to check on the young man."

"I've had bruises before, I'll be all right. Thank you, anyway for thinking of me," she told him.

"Get dressed and keep yourself warm or you'll end with pneumonia." He turned and left.

Well, thought Harriett, he seems to be seeing me more without any clothes on these days than he is with them on. I don't seem to have any effect on him in the least. And for some odd reason, she couldn't fathom out why, it made her feel sad.

She dressed and went to the blue room, tapped on the door. It was opened by Nicky and she entered. "How is he?" she whispered. "Is he still alive?"

"Only just, his breathing is very shallow but I think he'll make it."

"Does anyone know who he is?"

"No. It's a mystery. We'll just have to wait until he comes to. It's nearly lunchtime. Let's go and eat, there's nothing we can do here."

While they were sitting at the dining table Lord Planter said, "Have you seen the cottages? Jimmy's nearly finished the repairs and I'm most impressed with his work."

"I haven't been down to see him for a few weeks but I've seen the ones he's completed and they are looking much more habitable. He's a very good carpenter; it's something he likes doing but he's an all-rounder and I knew he would do a good job."

"Since he's made such a difference on the home farm I've been looking at The Manor. It's been really neglected for the past few years and some of the windows need replacing, in fact they could all do with replacing. The window frames are rotting in places, so when he's done down there I've a mind to set him to work up here. What do you think?"

"I think you're a very kind person, thank you."

"Good Lord, what's all that rot about?"

"You, keeping Jimmy in a job. I know he'll not be able to believe his luck but I thank you, for giving him a chance."

"There's nothing kind about it. He's a good worker and if I employ him it will be more cost effective than engaging an outsider, and they might not do such a good job as Jimmy. I've even been thinking about setting him up in business. The next time I go down to the farm I intend to have a look at that barn and see if it would make a good workshop for him. There are people I know who would buy furniture from him; good tradesmen are hard to come by these days. I thought we could go into partnership together. Set him up in the barn with the tools and equipment he'll need and put word out to anyone who wants any cabinets, tables, chairs etcetera, and we're in business. Once the cost of the equipment has been deducted, any profit can be equally shared. He will have a roof over his head and free working space for his labours and we will also profit for setting things up. We all win. Do you think he'll be interested in a partnership?"

"I think he'll snatch your hand of. If he doesn't, he's an idiot."

"Do you want to ask him or shall I?"

"Your idea, I think you should have the pleasure of asking him. He'd never believe me anyway," she laughed. Then in a serious voice she asked, "Do you think the young man upstairs will live?"

"There's a good chance. The doctor says we'll have to wait until his blood warms up and hope there's no damage to his internal organs, but he's young and his colour is a bit better than it was when we fished him out of the water. Do you want to go back up and keep an eye on him? The doctor is with him at the moment, but I don't think there's anything he can do so he might as well go. Let's go and see what he has to say."

They entered the bedroom and the doctor rose from the easy chair in front of the fire. "No change as yet, my lord, but at least he's still breathing and it's not as shallow as it was. It might be a good idea to try and get some chicken soup down him. If a few drops are placed in his mouth he should swallow it without choking; food and liquid, that might help."

"If there's nothing more to be done why not go home. We'll organize some soup for him and try to get something inside him. If you're needed again we'll send for you. Thank you for coming, Doctor Phillips."

The doctor didn't need telling twice, he collected his bag and went home.

Lord Planter rang the bell and Wrenshaw appeared. Lord Planter asked him to see if there was any soup available, and if so to bring up a bowl.

Lord Planter lifted the young man up while Harriett piled the pillows behind him so he was in a semi-sitting position and waited until the soup arrived. It wasn't chicken but vegetable, so Harriet ran down to the kitchen and collected another bowl and a sieve then ran back upstairs. She poured the soup through the sieve into the second bowl, then took the liquid over to the bed. Sitting on the edge, she placed a few drops between the young man's lips and she very slowly dripped the remainder into his mouth. By the end of half an hour the liquid was out of the bowl and inside the young man.

Harriett sat in the easy chair the doctor had vacated and read a book. By the time darkness fell there was still no sign of life from the young man, except the rise and fall of his chest was more pronounced and his colour was definitely improving.

At ten o'clock Lord Planter came into the room, checked the young man's pulse and said to Harriett, "Well his pulse is getting stronger, that's a good sign. I've asked for some warm milk to be brought up. I don't suppose it's any good telling Wrenshaw to drip the milk into the young man's mouth, is it?" He looked at Harriett. She shook her head. "No I didn't think so, but promise me, Hetty, when you've got the milk inside him you'll go to bed. There's nothing to be done now, it's up to him."

She nodded and said, "I will."

"Good, goodnight, Hetty." He left and she watched his back disappear behind the closed door.

True to her word Harriett managed to drip the warm milk into the young man and then she went to bed more than a little wearily. She undressed and put on a long cotton nightgown that fastened at the neck, then she climbed into bed. It didn't take long before she was sound asleep.

When she woke it was still dark. She didn't know how long she'd been asleep but she found herself tossing and turning and sleep wouldn't return. Harriett threw off the bedclothes and padded with bare feet out of her bedroom, along the corridor and into the blue room. She made her way over to the bed.

The young man was still sleeping. She reached out to feel his forehead and, to her surprise, his eyes opened and he grabbed her by the shoulders. "Sir David, thank God, the letter, in the shoulder pad, it's the servant." Then his hands dropped and he was once more lost to the world.

Harriett ran out of the bedroom, and without knocking she ran into Lord Planter's bedroom and over to his bed. She shook him by the shoulder to wake him up and he sat up abruptly making Harriett take a step back.

"Harriett, you startled me, are you all right, you look a bit shocked?"

"I am, but the young man… He woke up, he was rambling."

He lifted up the bedclothes and said, "Get in here where it's warm." He moved over to let her lay where he'd been lying. She felt the warm embrace of the bedclothes as Lord Planter covered her up. "Oh, that's nice." She snuggled down into the soft warm bed.

"What did he say?" he asked.

"Not much, he grabbed me and said, 'Sir David, thank God, the letter, in the shoulder pad, it's the servant'. Then he went back to sleep."

Lord Planter thought for a moment, before saying, "His clothes, Hetty, what happened to his clothes? Are they still down by the river where we took them off?"

"No, I bundled them up and pushed them between the wagon and the axle. There was a ledge. I forgot about them."

Lord Planter threw off the bedclothes and got out. Walking round to Harriett's side of the bed he proceeded to pull on his pants, then his jacket. "Stay here, Hetty, I won't be long."

Being left alone in Lord Planter's huge soft bed, Harriett pulled the bedclothes tightly round her neck and waited for the return of her husband.

Lord Planter returned bearing the bundle of wet clothes to find his wife fast asleep. He stood and looked down at her, letting all the love he felt for her pour out. There was nothing he would have liked more than to climb in bed beside her but he couldn't. He now knew who her father was and he had to travel to the city immediately. If he found what he was looking for in the shoulder pad of this young man's clothes, he had to go and see Sir David.

Kissing the first two fingers of his right hand he gently touched Harriett's cheek then he went down into the library carrying the wet clothes.

Taking them over to the fireplace he placed them in the hearth then went to his desk, got some scissors and proceeded to carefully cut the seam open of the first shoulder of the jacket, nothing there. He attacked the other side and, as he had expected he found a waterproof packet in place of the shoulder pad. He opened the packet to find a second oilskin and on opening this he found the letter. The seal was big and red with a crest on it; the seal was intact. The letter had not been opened.

His father had worked for the government. What office he never knew, but he can remember when he was about ten years old playing with a wooden horse and wagon he'd been given for his birthday on the landing at the top of the stairs, when the front door was opened by Wrenshaw (a much younger Wrenshaw) and Sir David Murray was admitted.

Sir David Murray was a much junior government employee who worked under his father and he had come, on a couple of occasions, to The Manor on government business. Lord Planter had taken particular notice of him because he had strawberry blond hair and it was the first time he had seen that colour hair on either man or woman. The same colour hair as Harriett. It fitted, it all fitted, that's why he'd thought he'd seen Harriett before. She even walked with a similar self-assured stride that Sir David had.

Sir David Murray worked for the government and the letter had a government seal on it. It had to be important if the young man went into the river to save it, if that's what happened, he could think of no other explanation. Even though the young man hadn't mentioned Sir David's second name, Lord Planter knew it had to be Sir David Murray.

He went over to the desk, took a sheet of paper and after a few seconds he began to write:

My darling Hetty,

When you read this letter I hope you're not going to be angry with me. I know this is your adventure but I must leave immediately for Drunbury and I have to leave you behind.

I will explain all when I get back, which will be sometime tomorrow I hope. I would have liked nothing more than to climb back in bed and lay by your side.

You looked so beautiful and peaceful I was loath to wake you. I leave you in charge of your fallen hero.

I must go now, my beautiful Hetty.

All my love, Nicky. XXX

He dusted some sand on it then folded it up, placed it in an envelope, addressed it to Lady Planter and took it upstairs, placing it on the bedside table for her to find when she woke that morning, for it was now one thirty a.m. With one last lingering look at his sleeping wife, Lord Planter headed for the stables.

He rode at a steady gallop. He had a five-hour ride ahead of him before he reached the city and was conscious of the government sealed letter inside his jacket. His greatcoat with seven shoulder capes fastened at the neck protected him against the cold night air. He stopped once at a wayside inn to have a bite to eat and give his horse a rest but was soon on his way again.

He knew Sir David Murray lived on the outskirts of Drunbury because his father had pointed it out on more than one occasion when they'd been returning to The Manor after staying at their townhouse in Drunbury. His journey went surprisingly quickly, hardly encountering any other rider until he neared the outskirts of the city.

He guessed the time to be nearly seven a.m. and, as the area became more built up he was pleased to see, as he neared Sir David's dwelling, a light on in a downstairs window.

Sir David had a reputation of being a recluse: he never attended any of the many invitations to parties or dinner evenings he received even when a young man. He was pursued by many a scheming mother with a daughter of marriageable age but still he remained a bachelor. He was well liked and respected in the government circles and held a high position of authority.

Lord Planter dismounted and tied up his horse, knocked on the door and waited.

After a few seconds the door was opened by a servant and Lord Planter said, "Could you tell Sir David that Lord Planter would be grateful if he could have a word with him?"

"Sir David doesn't receive visitors at his house. Please go to his office and make an appointment." The servant made to close the door.

Lord Planter put his foot in the door and said, "Please ask Sir David if he will see me. I'll wait here and if the answer is still 'no' I'll go away."

"Very well, my lord, if you would be kind enough to remove your boots you may wait inside. I will do as you request and ask Sir David." The servant waited until the boots were removed and Lord Planter stood in the hallway, bootless, then the servant closed the door.

The surprised servant opened the inner door and said, "Sir David will see you, come this way."

Lord Planter was shown into the breakfast room where he found Sir David eating breakfast. "You've grown," he remarked.

"Yes, it must be twenty years since I last saw you. I hope you're well, sir."

"I'm very well. Would you care to join me for breakfast?"

"I would indeed."

"Johnson, pull up a chair and get Lord Planter a plate. Why have you nothing on your feet?"

"Your servant asked me to remove my boots before I entered your house."

"I can only apologize to you for it. He is not under instructions to ask people to remove their footwear, but he is new to the position and seems to have one or two funny ideas of what is expected of him."

When Nicky was settled and a welcome plate of good hot food was placed in front of him, he looked across at Sir David and said, "It is of little consequence, Sir David, in fact my feet appreciate it. You may find this a very strange time to be calling, sir, but to be truthful, when I set out this morning I had no idea I would be calling to see you. I have a story to tell that you might find interesting."

"When did you set out?"

"About one thirty this morning."

"You've travelled from The Manor?"

"Yes, sir, from The Manor."

"It's a strange, not to mention dangerous time to be riding across the moors, surely?"

"It's a strange story, sir."

"You intrigue me, please begin."

"I know you are reputedly a recluse, Sir David, but no doubt you have heard I am married and how it all came about?"

"I had heard, you lost a bet or something and had to marry this peasant girl."

"That is roughly how it came about, but the very first time I saw my wife I thought I'd seen her before, of course I had not. Over the past seven months there have been a couple of instances when the feeling was repeated. I couldn't for the life of me figure out why I kept getting this feeling."

"The same feeling of recognition you mean?"

"Yes, but I know it to be impossible. Anyway to move on, have you heard of the Planter diamonds?"

"No, I can't say I have?"

"This set of jewellery was commissioned by my great grandfather. He married late in life and his bride was about twenty years his junior. He had this jewellery made especially for her. It consisted of a tiara, necklace, earrings, bangles and a ring, all worth a king's ransom. The day he went to collect them he was coming out of the jewellers and he saw his bride, entering a house belonging to a well-known rake. On further investigation it turned out that they were lovers, had been for years and she had married my great grandfather for his fortune. Needless to say she never knew about the jewels and they were placed in the bank and, it has been a rule of the family ever since, that the wife of the next generation of Planters would not be informed of the existence of this jewellery until their marriage had lasted twelve months and there was no sign of a hidden lover."

"I can understand this better than you think. I too have been betrayed by the fairer sex. This is why I have remained a bachelor."

"I had heard something about that, sir, but after you have heard my story you might feel quite differently."

"I doubt that very much, but you have my full attention, please carry on."

"Going back to this rule and the jewellery, no one more than me was surprised by my marriage. I have never found a female that took my fancy but I was aware I needed to get married and provide an heir. I could never bring myself to ask any of the social beauties I met to marry me. So there I was, bored out of my mind, doing my usual indifferent things. There didn't seem to be a purpose to anything in my life, so the beer was flowing nicely and I was challenged into a game of cards by this fat, unshaved, smelly man and I lost. He said I had to marry his daughter and because I was bored and well and truly in my cups I agreed. My friends all told me I was crazy and they didn't expect me to keep my word, the word of a drunk wasn't taken seriously. Anyway, I went ahead and married her. I left The Manor the next day. I couldn't bear to look at her for she was a sickly drab looking thing, forever passing out or being sick. About a week later I had a letter from my secretary telling me my wife had taken up a job, so I went home immediately to sort things out."

Lord Planter went on to tell his story to Sir David who listened intently and when Lord Planter had finished his story he asked, "What was the name of your wife's mother?"

"Lady Freda West."

"How old is your wife?"

"She's nearly twenty."

"You are thinking, your wife, is my daughter?"

"I am. It wasn't until I was approaching your house just now that I realised where I'd seen her before. It wasn't her I'd seen. It was you. I can remember playing with my toys on the landing at the top of the stairs when I was about ten years old and hearing a knocking on the door and you entering. I remember you distinctly because of the colour of your hair. I had never seen anyone with your hair colouring before and, at the age of ten you made an impression on me. I asked my father who you were and he said you worked for him at the government office. He also pointed out to me where you lived on a number of occasions when we'd passed your house."

"This is unbelievable."

"Yes, sir, I know, it's quite staggering. Is it possible, sir, that my wife could be your daughter?"

"Yes, it's possible. All these years I've thought that Freda betrayed me and all along she was carrying my child and I deserted her. I should have known she would never have let me down and gone off with someone else, we were so in love. In fact I loved her so much I could never look at another woman the same again. You say she's dead now?"

"I'm afraid so."

"She had a hard life?"

"Yes, sir, I think she had."

"Oh my poor Freda, what have I done?"

"You weren't to know, sir. I don't think she ever blamed you. She shielded you in fact. She wouldn't tell Harriett who her real father was because she said you might be married and have other children, and she didn't want to bring any trouble between you and your family."

"Does your wife know I'm her father?"

"No, I was on my way to my townhouse to grab a few hours' sleep, then to the bank to get the diamonds. As I said before, sir, it wasn't until I saw your house that the penny dropped. She will be the first Lady Planter to wear these jewels. There's been a sad line of disastrous marriages in my family but I'm hoping from now on things are going to get better. I was hoping to surprise her with them for her birthday, in two weeks. I left early this morning so she wouldn't know where I've been, hence the early morning ride."

"Do you love her?"

"Yes, sir, I do. She's turned out to be the best thing that's ever happened to me. She's given me a purpose in life. I feel alive. You'll love her, sir, I know you will. She is one exceptional young lady. She's only nineteen at the moment but she'll be twenty in two weeks' time."

"This Fat Man, you say he beat her?"

"He did, I'm sorry to say."

"Did he beat Freda?"

"Harriett says no, she thinks he loved her."

"At least that's something. You've picked a fine time to come to me with this story. I might be behind bars later this morning."

"Behind bars, you mean locked up?"

"I do, I was responsible for a letter, a very important letter. It was to be delivered to Colonel Bishop this morning, but my young apprentice talked me into letting him go and collect this letter. Against my better judgement I relented and he went to collect the letter to bring it back to me. He's the son of a good friend of mine and he's gone missing. The letter contains instructions for the movement of the army, and if this falls into the wrong hands it could cost our army many lives. What a fool I was, he was too young to be given such a responsibility and his family are devastated. I'll never forgive myself. I seem to cause bad luck to anyone I come into contact with. You'd better watch your back, young Nicky."

"Who is the young man?"

"Jacob Brightman. His father is Mr Ray Brightman. He's a lawyer. His wife, Mary Brightman, was a great friend of Freda's. We've remained friends, we never knew what happened to Freda, then we heard her father had committed suicide. Do you know Mr Ray Brightman?"

"No, it's not a name I've come across."

"Do you know I'm sick and tired of all this cloak and dagger stuff, I've had enough. If I'm still a free man after this morning's meeting I shall retire and go and live in my house in the country. I would dearly love to meet your wife. If I come out of this all right may I come with you when you go back to The Manor and see her? I wouldn't tell her I'm her father; I will leave that up to you."

Lord Planter was conscious of the servant hovering by the breakfast sideboard and remembered Harriett saying, 'It was the servant.' While the servant had his back to them Nicky put his finger to his lips and indicated with a slight nod in the servant's direction, and gently pulled at his lapel and looked down.

Sir David glanced at the open lapel and saw the corner of a white envelope, then Nicky let go of the lapel and the envelope was gone from sight. Sir David looked up at Nicky who gave the slightest of nods, then, taking up his napkin he quickly took out the envelope and wrapped the napkin round it, placing it on the table with his hand over it. He nodded to Sir David's napkin, which he slid across the table to Nicky, and Nicky slid the letter across to Sir David.

The servant turned and came over to them and asked, "Would there be anything else you require?"

"No thank you, that was most welcome, Sir David. I didn't expect to be eating my breakfast here. It has been nice to see you again after all these years. It must be a shock for you to learn you have a daughter."

"More than a shock, I still can't believe it. Is what you've just told me true, do I really have a daughter?"

"I think so, sir, but it would be best if you saw her for yourself and made up your own mind. If, once you've seen her you decide you don't want anything to do with her, then she need never know. It will be your decision."

"I must leave. I have to be at the chambers for this meeting with the colonel. What do you intend to do now?"

"I was heading for my townhouse to grab a few hours' sleep before I go to the bank, then head back to The Manor. I would like to know the outcome of the missing letter before I leave Drunbury. May I call on you on my way back home?"

"You might turn out to be my son-in-law. Why don't you stay here? John will show you up to one of the guest bedrooms then, as soon as I know, I'll let you know."

"I confess to not relishing getting back on my horse for another half hour's ride. Do you have room to stable and feed my horse?"

"I do." He turned to the servant and said, "John, would you have Lord Planter's horse taken to the stables, and see to it that's its fed and watered after you've shown him to his room?"

"Very good, sir. If you'd like to follow me, my lord," John gave a slight bow in Nicky's direction.

Nicky followed the servant up the wide curving staircase and along the long landing. Glancing down Nicky saw Sir David hurriedly tuck the envelope inside his jacket pocket, then wipe his mouth with the napkin before leaving the breakfast table.

Not bothering to get undressed, Nicky took off his jacket and lay down on top of the bed. It wasn't long before he felt himself drifting off to sleep.

CHAPTER 11

Harriett slowly shook off sleep and gave a long stretch. Opening her eyes it took her a few seconds to remember where she was. She remembered coming into Lord Planter's bedroom and climbing into his bed. She remembered relating to him what the young man had said to her and Lord Planter getting up and leaving the room; that's the last she can remember. There was no sign of him now in the bedroom.

She looked across at the closed curtains; she could see it was daylight through a gap at the side. She got up, went across the room and threw back the curtains. Although it was daylight it was grey and overcast much as it had been the day before.

She was about to head back to her own bedroom when the envelope, propped up on the side table caught her eye.

It was addressed to her in big bold letters. She had never had a letter in her life, so she took it back to her own bedroom. Sitting on the edge of the bed she very carefully opened it.

Harriett read the contents three times before she accepted that the letter was for her. If she was not mistaken, Lord Planter had left her a love letter. He had written, 'My darling Hetty' and called her his 'beautiful Hetty'. He had wanted to get back in bed with her and what had she done? SLEPT THROUGH IT. What had he to tell her? He had left her in charge of the young man. She folded the letter and put it back in its envelope. She got dressed then put the letter into her dress pocket.

Harriett walked along the corridor to the sick room and gently tapped on the door.

"Come in," called a man's voice.

Harriett opened the door to find the young man sitting up in bed.

"It's about time someone came. Where am I?" asked the young man.

"In a better place than you were when we found you," replied Harriett.

"Beg pardon, but I've been awake for hours and I haven't seen a soul. Where am I?" he asked again.

"You're at Lord Planter's home, The Manor in Lightbridge."

"Lightbridge, but that's miles away."

"Miles away from where?" she wanted to know.

"Why, Drunbury of course."

"Well, you got that right. Would you like something to eat?"

"I'll say I would, I'm devilishly hungry."

Harriett went to the head of the bed and pulled the bell cord and Wrenshaw appeared. "Wrenshaw, could you please arrange for some breakfast to be sent up for the invalid."

"Invalid, I ain't an invalid you know," complained the young man.

"Of course you are. You've been unconscious for about twenty-four hours."

"Twenty-four hours? Where are my clothes? I have to be somewhere by nine o'clock this morning."

"Well it's too late for that now, it's past ten."

"I need my clothes, where are my clothes?"

"The last time I saw them they were bundled up and placed under the wagon."

"What wagon?"

"The wagon we used to bring you back here."

"Why don't I remember any of this? Did you drug me?"

"Drug you, what sort of question is that? We risked life and limb to save you and you accuse us of drugging you. You are a very ungrateful young man."

"Look, I'm sorry but it's very important I have my clothes and what's this about you risking life and limb?"

A knock came to the door and Sally walked in bearing a tray with bacon and eggs, some chunks of bread and a cup of tea. While he ate Harriett told him how he'd become Lord Planter's guest. He remembered being set upon when he was on his way to see Sir David with the letter. He'd badgered Sir David into letting him travel to the army barracks at Nontum and pick up a letter to deliver to Sir David's house.

He had been set upon by two men. One he recognised as the servant at Sir David's house, the other was unknown to him. He'd managed to break free and flee, but he knew they were after him so he ran down towards the river hoping to cross the bridge further downstream. It had been raining and he lost his footing and fell into the river. He remembered being swept along with the current and he could feel himself getting colder and colder, but the current was too strong for him and it kept on taking him downstream. He had felt something knock into him and had found himself floating

144

beside a tree, also being swept along. So he'd climbed onto it and that was the last he could remember.

Harriett sat looking at him and asked, "How did you come to be in the river?"

"I slipped and fell in."

"Is that it, you just slipped and fell in?"

"What else could it be?"

"I don't know but something's going on. Can't you remember waking up in the early hours of the morning and calling me Sir David?"

"I did no such thing."

"You did. Who's Sir David?"

The young man, not wanting to admit to knowing Sir David, or anything about the government letter, replied, "How the devil should I know, I've never heard of him. What else did I say?"

"You deny saying anything. Why would you want to know what else you said if you didn't say anything and you don't know Sir David?"

Their conversation was interrupted by the reappearance of Wrenshaw, who came in and asked if the young man had finished with his breakfast and he removed the tray and left the room.

"Would you mind giving me an hour to get washed and dressed? Then I would like to see about leaving. Did you say this house belongs to Lord Planter?"

"You may certainly have an hour to freshen up but there are no clothes for you to get dressed in. I'm afraid you will have to wait until Lord Planter gets back this evening and ask if you may borrow some of his clothes. It looks like you're stranded here for the time being."

Harriett went to her bedroom but left the door open so she could hear if the young man left his room. There was something fishy about him. First he denied calling her Sir David, but a flush had come to his cheeks and Harriett knew he had been telling her lies. His insistence on having his clothes back, even though he must know they were ruined, also made Harriett suspicious.

Nicky had been interested in the young man's clothes. He'd asked her what happened to them and when she told him, he left the bedroom. Nicky had told her to keep an eye on the young man and that was what she intended to do, there was nothing else for it.

An hour later she knocked on the young man's door again and entered. She had decided to sit with him and see if she could get anything more out of him but, when she entered his bedroom, she found him fast asleep again.

Sitting in the chair by the fireside, Harriett took out her letter and she sat reading it. She read it through more than once and each time she still came to the same conclusion. It was a love letter. Could it be possible he had come to love her? She finally admitted to herself she had come to love him. He was the most wonderful man in the world.

When Harriett thought she might have to leave The Manor, her despair was so deep she felt panic. Never to see Nicky again was her most dreaded fear. Sometimes she felt so guilty about marrying him. She'd thought about asking him to set her up in a little cottage of her own with enough money to live on, then he could go his own way and forget about her but, the thought of never seeing him again broke her heart.

Harriett had come to respect and admire Nicky, to say nothing of the desire she felt for him. Instead of being embarrassed when he'd walked into her bedroom while she was naked and saw the look in his eyes, it sent her heart racing. She had liked the feeling, as he looked her up and down.

The young man woke and saw Harriett sitting, reading a letter and he asked, "What are you reading?"

Harriett guiltily hid her letter down the side of her chair and blushing she said, "Nothing."

"You were you know, I saw you."

"Even if I was, it's none of your business."

"Why did you look so guilty when I asked you what you were reading?"

"Guilty! Why should I be guilty, it's my letter and I'll read it if I want to."

"Where are my clothes?" he demanded.

"Why do you want them?"

"I need to get dressed and be on my way."

"You're not fit to travel."

"Am I a prisoner?"

"Prisoner? What are you talking about?"

"You seem to be trying to keep me here."

"You've been very poorly, you need to rest."

"Are you sure I've only been here since yesterday morning?"

"Of course I am. Why, how long do you think you've been here?"

"I don't know, you could have drugged me. I could have been here weeks. They'll be looking for me you know."

"Good, I hope they find you, whoever they are, and take you off my hands. What's your name by the way?"

"Why do you want to know?"

"What's the matter with you? Are you some sort of spy or something? Why are you being so secretive?"

The young man had the grace to blush and told her, "My name's Jacob Brightman."

"You are a spy."

"Don't talk ridiculous, what flights of fancy have got into your top loft."

"What's my top loft?"

"Your brain, if you have one."

"Do you know, Jacob Brightman, you are a very rude young man and I don't want anything more to do with you. I shall tell Wrenshaw to bring you something to eat, and if he has any trouble with you before Lord Planter gets back then he has to tie you to the bed." She haughtily left the room and made her way down to the sitting room.

Harriett rang the bell and Wrenshaw appeared. "Wrenshaw, will you have some food sent up for the invalid and then will you send for Roy?"

Wrenshaw bowed slightly and said, "Very good, my lady."

"And, Wrenshaw, if the young man asks you for any clothes, please don't give him any."

"Very good, my lady."

"Do you know what happened to the young man's clothes?"

"I believe Sarah found them in the hearth in the library and has taken them to be laundered."

"Thank you, will you ask Sarah to come and see me as well?"

"Very good, my lady." He quickly left the room in case he was asked to do anything else.

Sarah, the object of Jimmy's passion, knocked gently on the sitting room door. She had never been asked to be seen by Lady Planter. She was happy to come to work then go home. She was nervous about being summoned. She knew Lady

Planter was Jimmy's friend and she wondered if Jimmy had told her they wanted to get married.

"Come in," Harriett called and a young maid entered. "You must be Sarah?"

Sarah gave a little curtsey and said, "Yes, my lady."

"Where are the clothes you found in the hearth this morning?"

"They are being dried, my lady. They were very smelly and wet so Mrs Raynor gave instructions for them to be washed. I think the jacket needed repairing too; the seams had come away on both shoulders."

"When they're ready, would you please bring them to me?"

"Very well, my lady. Will that be all?"

"Yes, thank you."

When Sarah opened the door to leave, Roy was about to knock so she waved him in and told him to close the door. "Roy, Lord Planter said you did bare-knuckle fighting. Well I think I need you and your bare knuckles."

"Yes, but unofficially, my lady."

"Oh yes, anyway that's not important, Roy, I shall not tell anyone. I think we have a spy in the house and I would like you to keep an eye on him. I think he might try to escape. Lord Planter should be home sometime this evening and I'd hate for the young man to disappear before he gets home."

Roy looked at Lady Planter. Things had certainly livened up since she'd come to The Manor. "A spy you say, what sort of a spy?"

"How many sorts are there?"

"Well there's spies that try to get the country's secrets and sell them to make money. Then there's spies that spy on people to try and find out things about them that they'd rather nobody

149

knew about, and then they blackmail them. That's two types of spies for a start. This young man you're talking about, is he selling the country's secrets or is he spying on Lord Planter or you?"

Harriett thought for a moment. "I don't know but if we work backwards, I don't think he can be spying on either Lord Planter or me because he had no way of knowing that we would fish him out of the river. It was flowing too fast, and if that tree he'd climbed onto hadn't got stuck on the bend, then he could be well out to sea by now, so it must be the country's secrets."

"That's logical, I can see your point. What do you want me to do exactly?"

"I thought you could go and sit with him and keep him company until Lord Planter returns and make sure he doesn't escape. If he tries to, you can always punch him, you know, with your bare knuckles."

"Well, it's a plan I suppose."

"You can keep him occupied by telling him tales about your fights, I'm sure that would take his mind off spying. I was going to tell Wrenshaw to tie him to the bed but I don't think Wrenshaw is cut out for that sort of thing, do you?"

Roy laughed. "Poor Wrenshaw, from negroes to spies, his quiet life has turned upside down. I'd better get off then and make sure the spy doesn't escape."

Roy liked Lady Planter, but he didn't for one minute think that the young man upstairs was a spy, after all they weren't in the middle of a war.

Jacob was just about to climb out of bed when the door opened and in walked a young man dressed like one of the stable hands back home. "Who are you?" he demanded.

"I've come to keep you company until Lord Planter arrives. Can you play cards?" asked Roy.

"Of course I can, but I want my clothes. Go fetch me my clothes," the young man demanded.

"Sorry, can't do that, under orders to keep you here until Lord Planter arrives," replied Roy enjoying himself immensely.

"I'm not a prisoner you know. Why can't I have my clothes?"

"I've no idea; I know nothing about your clothes."

"Well fetch someone who does."

"My, you're a rude young man, who taught you your manners?"

"Look, it's most important that I leave here immediately but I need my clothes. I can't go around the countryside in my underwear."

"I think if you have a good look, it's not even your underwear."

Jacob pulled up the sheets and looked down, and right enough they weren't his drawers.

"Where's the young lady that was here before? Fetch her, she seems to know more about this than anyone."

"You're very good at handing out orders, mate, but I don't answer to you. My instructions are to keep an eye on you until…"

"Yes, yes I know, until Lord Planter arrives," interrupted the young man.

"We could have a game of cards to pass the time."

"I don't want to play cards. I want to get dressed in my own clothes and leave."

"Have you any transport?"

"No."

"So you have no transport but you intend to leave here and make your way over a moor you don't know, until you arrive somewhere, where you can ask someone where you are." Roy nodded and added, "Some plan that is. You'll not last half a day out on the moor, you'll find yourself at the bottom of a bog and that will be that."

Jacob gave up, he was too tired to argue any more. It was too late to deliver the letter anyway but he had to know that it was safe so he needed his clothes. He laid his head back and closed his eyes.

In the sitting room Harriett called, "Come in."

Sarah entered the sitting room with the dried clothes and said, "As you requested, the young man's clothes, dried and repaired, my lady."

"Thank you, Sarah. That will be all."

If the two shoulder seams had been re-sewn that must mean that Nicky had found whatever had been hidden there, so she decided to take the clothes up to Jacob and see what happened. She tapped on the door and went in bearing the laundered clothing.

Roy had been playing solitaire but he jumped up when Harriett entered. "All's quiet, Lady Planter. He's fallen asleep."

"What do you make of him, Roy? Do you think he's a spy?"

"No, I don't think so. He looks and acts like the gentry, giving orders out left right and centre and expecting them to be obeyed. I don't think a spy would act like that, not that I know much about spies. I've never come across one as far as I know. But I think a spy would try to work his way into your confidence, not get your back up."

Harriett thought about that for a few seconds. "Yes, I think you may be right about that, he certainly got my back up."

"And mine."

"It looks like a false alarm then, Roy, but thank you for stepping in for me, I appreciate it."

"Any time you need anything, Lady Planter, I'm your man." He grinned and she laughed at him and he went back to the stables.

Harriett went and sat in the armchair, took out her prized letter and started reading it again, while she waited for the young man to wake up.

Lord Planter felt his shoulder being shaken and he opened his tired eyes to see the same servant that had served him breakfast standing over him. "Sorry to wake you, my lord, but you're wanted in the library."

"What time is it?"

"Half past ten, my lord."

"Is Sir David back already?"

"He is, my lord, and accompanied by some Bow Street Runners."

"Very well, I'll be down directly."

Nicky went over to the washstand and splashed cold water on his face, and after putting on his jacket and pulling on his boots he made his way down to the library.

When he entered he was met by Sir David, who said, "Lord Planter, this is Colonel Bishop and these two gentlemen are constables from the Bow Street Runners. Colonel Bishop would very much like to hear your story of how you came by the letter."

Nicky held out his hand and shook hands with the colonel. "Not much to tell really, Colonel Bishop. My wife saw a young man lying across a floating tree that had become lodged in a bend in the river. We pulled him out and took him home. He was very cold and unconscious so we put him to bed with lots of bed warmers and waited. We did not know the young man. My wife went to check on him just after midnight and he woke up and said, 'Sir David, thank God, the letter, in the shoulder pad, it's the servant', then passed out again. My wife came and told me.

"My father worked for the government, and when I was a little boy I had seen and heard about Sir David who had worked for my father. Knowing Sir David to be a government official and the young man muttering about shoulder pads and servants, plus the unconventional way the young man came to be my guest, I put two and two together. I got the clothes he had worn, cut the stitching across the shoulders and found an oilskin in place of one of the shoulder pads. I unwrapped the oilskin, found a second oilskin, and inside this second oilskin was a letter perfectly dry and bearing the government seal. I could see that the seal hadn't been broken, so I decided to set off for Drunbury to Sir David's house. I concocted a story while I rode because of the young man saying it was the servant. I didn't know what he meant by that, but I couldn't risk speaking openly in front of any of Sir David's servants, not knowing any of them. I thought it better to be safe than sorry, and that's all I can tell you."

"You mean the story about me having a daughter was all made up?" asked Sir David.

"Sorry, no, not that part, that part is perfectly true. I believe that my wife is your daughter. The bit I made up was the bit about the Planter diamonds. There are no diamonds I'm sorry to say. Everything else is perfectly true."

"What about the young man?" the colonel asked.

"That I don't know either, sir. He was unconscious when I left but his colour was much more normal and his breathing was much better, and if he had come round for a few seconds to tell my wife about the shoulder pads, I think he may be all right."

"That was very quick thinking on your part, Lord Planter. The letter contained the army's movements and although we are not at war it's something we don't want spread about. These two gentlemen are here to take Sir David's servant into custody and try to find out who he is working for." The colonel held out his hand again to Nicky and added, "Nice to have met you, young man, and many thanks, it is most appreciated."

When they had gone Nicky asked, "Which servant is it?"

"It can only be one, and he was serving at breakfast. All my other servants have been with me for years. He's only been here about three months." Sir David continued, "I must go and see Ray and Mary Brightman and tell them their son is found. They are very much distressed, as was I. Would you like to come with me and reassure them?"

"I'll come with pleasure if you think it will help."

"I do, I'm still trying to come to terms with the fact I have a daughter and that my poor Freda is no longer with us. If I give my servants instructions to pack my bag, would it be an intrusion if I were to come back with you to see both Jacob and my daughter?"

"It would be a pleasure to have your company, Sir David."

"David will do, my boy. After all you are my son-in-law and I hope we will deal well together."

"I hope so too, sir."

Nicky followed Sir David up two flights of wooden stairs to the top floor of a building that looked to contain various offices. The door they entered had 'Ray Brightman, Lawyer' written on it in big black letters.

"David, is there any news?" asked the well-dressed man sitting behind a huge desk cluttered with papers.

"Lord Planter, Mr Ray Brightman." They shook hands and Sir David continued, "There is indeed. Jacob is safe at Lord Planter's manor – he was pulled out of the river. Lord Planter thinks he's going to be all right. He was very poorly when Lord Planter left this morning, but improving."

"Thank God for that. Does Mary know?"

"No, we came straight here. I thought you might like to be the one to tell her, as you took all the blame for letting him come to work for me in the first place."

"I'll get my coat."

Mary Brightman was a middle-aged woman who didn't look her years. She had a straight back and well-shaped body, but sad eyes. She stood looking out of the window wondering where her son was. Something bad must have happened to him, for he would never have let her worry by staying out all night without letting her know. Since he had gone to work in the Government Security Department she never stopped worrying about him. Maybe she was over protective but he was all she had.

Her husband had betrayed her with another woman and it had broken her heart. She had loved him with every fibre of her being and she has never forgiven him. She dare not trust him again because she never wanted to be hurt like that again.

The door opened and Mary turned round to see the object of her thoughts walking up to her, with Sir David Murray behind him and another gentleman she did not know. "Is it bad news?" she whispered.

"On the contrary, he's been found, Mary. He's at Lord Planter's manor."

"Is he all right?" she asked, holding out a trembling hand to Sir David.

"We hope so, Mary. He was much improved when Lord Planter left."

"What's the matter with him?"

"I've given instructions for our bags to be packed. We're setting off as soon as our boxes are on the coach, so go and get ready and we'll hear all about it while we're on our way," her husband said.

CHAPTER 12

Harriett was sitting reading her letter when she heard, "You're back are you?" She hastily folded her letter and pocketed it.

The young man's clothes were hanging behind the door. "There you are, your clothes cleaned, dried and mended." She pointed to the door. The young man bounded out of bed and grabbed the clothes. The first thing he did was check the shoulder pad. "You'll find nothing there, whatever it was you had hidden is gone," Harriett told him.

"I didn't have anything hidden," he denied.

"You did," she countered.

"I did not."

"I know you did, you told me so in the early hours of this morning."

"I don't believe you."

"How did I know to tell Lord Planter where to look then?"

He fell silent at this, got back in bed and lay back on his pillow.

"You don't have to worry. I'm sure Lord Planter has it all in hand."

"You have a lot of faith in this Lord Planter."

"If it hadn't been for him you wouldn't be here now."

"I'm much obliged to him, I'm sure, but I really do need to go. It's very important I get to Drunbury as soon as possible. I was on important business and my mother will be worried sick by now. I need to let her know I'm all right."

"Well, at least you care about somebody else, besides yourself."

"I really do appreciate what you've done for me but it's the letter you see, it was important and now it's gone. Are you sure it's not the one you keep reading, then hiding away when you know I'm watching you?"

"What would I want with your precious letter? I shouldn't worry too much about it if I were you. If Lord Planter has the letter, he'll know what to do with it."

"*If*, he has the letter. Don't you know? How can he know what to do with it? I was on government business and I've let everybody down. I don't know what Sir David will think of me. I badgered him into letting me go for the letter instead of him. Now I have not only let him down, I may have got him into serious trouble too. Did Lord Planter know who I was?"

"I'm afraid not."

"Then how can he have known where to deliver the letter to? That's if he actually has the letter. Did you see it?"

"No, I fell asleep and he was gone by the time I woke up."

"You fell asleep! How could you fall asleep when all this excitement is going on under your nose? So what you're telling me is that you don't know for certain he has the letter?"

"Let me tell you this. I had been through a very busy day yesterday, to say nothing of throwing myself in a swollen, freezing river to rescue you. That's why I fell asleep. I woke up at one o'clock in the morning and got out of my nice warm bed to see if you were all right, and yes, you were, you were cosy and warm and fast asleep without a care in the world. No, I do not know if my husband got the letter, but he went to collect your clothes early this morning and they were found in the hearth, wet and smelly. The maid took them and had them laundered. Both the shoulder seams of your jacket were cut open, and as there was only Lord Planter who knew where your clothes were, and that the letter was in one of the shoulder pads, he must found it. He was gone when I woke up this morning. I think he's gone to deliver the letter. He had a look of realization on his face when I mentioned Sir David, so he might have taken the letter on to him."

"Lord, I do hope so. What a stupid time to fall asleep."

"No more stupid than falling into a raging river with a government letter sewn into your jacket."

"It was a very good hiding place."

"That's if the letter survived a good soaking and didn't get into the wrong hands."

Jacob heaved a big sigh and lay back on the pillow once more. "I'm sorry, it's just that I'm worried sick. I really do appreciate the fact that you saved my life. I can't thank you enough for rescuing me. Did you really jump in the river to rescue me?"

"Yes, I did. Lord Planter was going to go in after you but I pointed out to him that it would be best if he kept hold of me, because there was no way I could keep a hold of him, and, to be honest, there wasn't any time to argue, we just got on with it. Look, get dressed and come down to the dining room and have something to eat. It's nearly time for dinner; you'll feel much better when you've eaten something."

Dinner was over and Harriett and Jacob retired to the library where a fire had been lit. Jacob was perusing the books along the shelves when they heard a carriage arrive, then voices in the hall.

The library door opened and Lord Planter stood holding the door open. A smart lady dressed in a long maroon coat and maroon and black hat entered, closely followed by two tall gentlemen. One had jet-black hair and the other, older gentleman, very pale sandy-coloured hair, greying at the sides.

Jacob rushed forward and hugged the lady. "Mother! I'm so pleased to see you."

She returned his embrace and said, "And I you."

Jacob then went over to shake hands with the black-haired gentleman. "Father."

"Jacob, how are you, my boy?" and, ignoring the outstretched hand, his father grabbed him and pulled him into a loving hug.

"I say, sir, steady on. Much better for seeing you. And you, Sir David, I'm so sorry for all the trouble I've caused you. Did you get the letter?" He shook hands with the other gentleman.

"Yes Jacob, I got the letter. It is delivered safely, thanks to Lord Planter and, I think, this young lady." Sir David went across the room and took both of Harriett's hands in his and smiled down at her. "You've had quite an adventure, I hear."

"Yes, sir, I have, it's been most exciting. Only I had Jacob down as a spy but it turns out he's not a spy after all," she replied.

"You thought Jacob was a spy," he laughed.

"I did, and so would you have if you'd seen how secretive he was, how he kept on and on about wanting his clothes."

"That's a good one coming from you. What about you and that letter you keep reading, over and over again if you thought nobody was looking, then trying to hide it as though you had a guilty secret? I thought it was my letter you had found. Then keeping me a prisoner and acting like a jailer. It was you who acted like a spy."

Harriett went across to the mirror and stood looking at herself.

"What are you looking at now?" Jacob wanted to know.

"I'm looking to see if I look anything like a spy."

"Why, what does a spy look like?" asked Jacob.

"I don't know, but not like me."

Sir David couldn't keep a straight face and he burst out laughing.

Lord Planter closed the door and came into the room. Going over to Harriett, he took her hands. "Have you been having a bad time of it while I've been away?"

"Not at all. I got Roy to sit in the bedroom with Jacob in case he tried to escape. When I took Jacob's clean clothes up, Roy said he didn't think he was a spy so he went back to the stables."

Lord Planter smiled down at her and said, "I'm pleased you've been putting the servants to good use." Then he let go of her hand and turned to Jacob. "I'm pleased to see you in such good health after the scare you gave us all."

Jacob held out his hand and said, "I'm in excellent health, Lord Planter. I think it's you I have to thank for saving my life."

"On the contrary, it's my wife you have to thank. She saw you in the river and it was she that plunged into the raging water to get you out."

Jacob shot a glance at Harriett and with a red face mumbled, "Much obliged," then continued addressing Nicky, "You found the letter?"

"I did, only after Harriett came in to tell me what you'd said to her. I knew Sir David from when he worked for my father so I knew he worked for the government. Once I had found the letter with the government seal on it, I knew it must be important so off I went to see Sir David. So you see, all is well."

Jacob said, "I thought the letter Lady Planter kept reading was my letter because every time I came round she was reading it. When I spoke she'd hurriedly hide the letter down the side of the chair or stuff it into her pocket. What else could it have been but my letter?"

Harriett cast her eyes in Nicky's direction only to find he was looking at her with a knowing smile on his lips, which made her blush. To hide her embarrassment, she was nettled into saying to Jacob, "If I'd known you were going to turn out to be such a telltale I'd have left you to float away down river."

"I ain't no telltale," snapped Jacob. "If I'd been a telltale I'd have told the footpads where the letter was and I wouldn't have ended up in the river. It was dashed cold in that water."

"I'm well aware of that, thank you. I bet you can't remember Lord Planter having to strip you off and cover you in blankets to keep you warm either, can you?" Harriett snapped back.

"You let her see me naked?" he demanded of Nicky.

"Had to, we had to get you warm and dry as soon as possible. It could have meant life or death leaving you in wet clothes, it was much more sensible to wrap you up in dry blankets on the journey home. Had to be done I'm afraid," Nicky replied.

"There wasn't much to see anyway," Harriett confirmed.

"What was all the secrecy about her letter, that's what I want to know?" said a highly flushed Jacob trying to change the subject.

Having seen the look that had passed between Lord and Lady Planter his mother said soothingly, "I think, Jacob, it might have been a love letter. That's what we women like to do, read our love letters when no one's watching."

"A love letter!" said Jacob in disgust. "What would Lady Planter be doing having a love letter? She's married."

"One doesn't necessarily preclude the other, Jacob. If the love letter was from someone other than Lord Planter, I think you may have landed Lady Planter in deep trouble," his mother told him.

Jacob looked at his mother open mouthed, realising the awkward position he had landed his hostess in and he stammered, "Beg pardon, Lady Planter, I didn't mean to cause you any trouble."

Mrs Brightman said to Harriett, "Lady Planter, there are no words that can express my thanks for what you did for my son. Now I've seen he's all right with my own eyes would you mind very much if I went to bed? It's been a long emotional day and I'm not as young as I used to be."

Lord Planter went over to the fireplace and rang the bell.

"Of course we don't mind. Is there anything I can get you?"

"A glass of warm milk would be very nice."

Wrenshaw entered the room and Lord Planter said, "Have Mr and Mrs Brightman shown up to their room and have some warm milk and a bite to eat sent up, oh, and a whisky for Mr Brightman."

"Very good, my lord."

"Before you retire, Ray, what time do you intend to return to Drunbury tomorrow? I would very much appreciate a lift back if it's not too much trouble. I know you're a very busy man and I also have a few loose ends to tie up," Sir David told them.

"Early, I was intending to stay another day but as my son seems to be back in good health, I think we'd better get him back home. Lord and Lady Planter have already been too kind." He smiled. "If it's all right with you, Lord Planter, I should like to set off around nine o'clock in the morning. I left quite a few things unattended to this morning. I don't have to tell you how much we appreciate what you've done for us. All I can say is, thank you, from the bottom of my heart."

"Nonsense, think nothing of it, we only did what anyone would have done under the circumstances. I'll tell Wrenshaw to arrange breakfast to be served at eight, but you are more than welcome to stay. I'm just thankful things have worked out all right for everybody, especially you, young man." He looked across at Jacob. "Don't go falling into any more rivers and giving your poor mother any more frights."

"I'll try my best, sir. I say, I hope I haven't caused any trouble between you and Lady Planter over that letter have I?" Jacob asked.

"I think we can overcome any difficulty there might be over the love letter, Jacob. Don't worry your head over it," Nicky assured him.

Before Sir David followed the others upstairs, he said to Nicky, "About that other thing, regarding the discussion we had earlier this morning. Please feel free to tell Harriett I am her father. I think it would be best coming from you."

"Very well, I'll do my best." Nicky smiled.

When Nicky and Harriett were left alone, Harriett was trying to cover up her embarrassment and Nicky was wondering where to begin.

"Come and sit down, Harriett, we have things to talk about."

Harriett's heart sank. Nicky's face and voice were so grave that she had a premonition he was going to tell her he wanted her to leave. She was not unaware of the trouble she'd caused him since she came into his life and she was dreading what he had to say. She sat in the corner of the sofa with her hands clasped tightly together and her eyes downcast.

Nicky sat in the opposite corner of the sofa and, leaning forward, he rested his elbows on his knees so he couldn't see her face. He was going to tell her he knew who her father was and if she wanted to, she could go and live with him if she was unhappy here. She had become so much part of his life he didn't want to lose her. He didn't want to go back to his old way of life idling it away. He didn't think he could live without her now he had found her.

The silence was deafening and Harriett was sure Nicky could hear her heart pounding.

After a few seconds Nicky broke the silence by beginning. "I know our relationship didn't get off to a very good start. In fact I am aware of your dislike and disgust of me and if I'm truthful, I can't blame you. Every time I think of you being beaten because of me, I'm disgusted with myself. Over these past seven months, Harriett, I've come to regard you with respect, admiration and love. I have fallen head over heels in love with you. I know you're only nineteen and I'm nearly thirty, you should be with someone nearer your own age. I've tried not to want you so much but it will not do. I lie in bed at night knowing you are just across the hallway, and especially since seeing you naked, you obsess my mind, Hetty.

"Before I met you I had lived a life very much without emotion. My father was a very hard, indifferent man and my mother tolerated me. I grew up having anything I wanted except love. My father never asked me to help around the farm because everything I did was not good enough for him, so I joined the Army. I went to the Peninsular for three years and that's how I met Tandy, Captain Grey and Captain Lally. Captain Grey was the captain of the ship going out and Captain Lally on the way back.

"My mother died when I was only nine years old and my father died while I was abroad.

"I will not lie to you, Hetty. I've been with many women over the years, but I never had any feelings for any of them. In fact all the girls I knew were either after a husband, or they were after my money.

"Then you come into my life, I had feelings I'd long since forgotten, shock at being the cause of your beatings, and disbelief that I could have let things slide here at The Manor the way I had. The way I'd let that creep Meanwood swindle me out of all that money, amusement at some of the things you do and say, pride when I go down to the home farm and see how much has been achieved over the past few months and most of all love, love for a beautiful young woman with a heart of gold.

"But with love comes uncertainty. If you rejected my advances and told me you didn't want anything to do with me I don't know what I would do. I can't bear the thought of never seeing you again or that you find me repulsive. This is why I am finding it very difficult to explain to you.

"Things came to a head the night you came into my bedroom to tell me young Jacob had called you Sir David. As soon as you said that name, I knew who your father was. Sir David used to come here when he was a young man and I was a boy. I used to see him when he came to see my father. I knew he was in government so, when you said his name and mentioned letters in shoulder pads and the young man floating in the river, I put two and two together. When I came back from the stable last night after going to fetch the clothes, you were fast asleep. In my bed! God, what I would have given to creep in beside you and watch you sleep like I did when we took Reco to Berkwash.

"I found the letter and went to see Sir David. You'd said Jacob said it was the servant. I didn't know which servant so I told Sir David about how you became my wife and who your mother was. I told him what you'd said about The Fat Man not being your father, and how the father of the baby your mother was carrying was turned away, and she was forced to marry The Fat Man. He was shocked, but he knew he was your father. He knew when I was telling him the story it was about him and your mother. He said he wanted to come and meet you and if you wanted to go and live with him he would be delighted to have you. I told him if he decided he didn't want you to know he was your father once he'd met you, all he had to do was tell me and it would remain our secret. But as soon as he met you, he knew he wanted you to know about him.

"It's your decision, Harriett. Stay with me or go and live with Sir David." He sat with his back to her, head down waiting for her reply.

What came next was the last thing he expected to hear. "If you do that thing again and I still like it, I'll let you see my graze."

He turned and looked at her. "What thing?"

She reached out her hand and ran her finger gently over his lips then did the same to hers. "That thing."

Nicky's heart started beating so fast he could hardly breathe. He grabbed her wrist and pulled her to her feet, dragging her up the stairs after him.

After he had closed the bedroom door, he took her by the shoulders and said, "I must warn you, Hetty, I've been celibate since we've been married, so once I start I won't be able to stop."

"What does celibate mean?"

Nicky shook his head and said, "My God, Hetty, I love you so much. I didn't think I was capable of feeling like this. Celibate, my darling, means I haven't had sex with a woman since we've been married."

"Good, I'm pleased to hear it."

"Hetty, I don't think you fully understand the implication of what I am saying."

"And I don't think you understand the implication of what I am saying. Yes, I did resent you when I was forced into marriage but the resentment came, I think, from the fact you were blaming me for what happened. Since we've come to know each other better the resentment turned to respect, and I return your love, Nicky, I think you're wonderful. I don't want to go and live with Sir David. I want to say here with you, please don't send me away."

"Oh, my darling Hetty," he said undoing the buttons of her gown and adding, "Let's try that thing out shall we," and his lips headed for hers.

Ray looked over at his wife with concern. She was standing, looking out of the window with her arms folded across her chest as if holding herself in. She had her back to him; he was unable to see her face.

"Mary, are you all right?" he asked softly. "It's not like you to admit to feeling tired."

Mary was silent for a few seconds then she turned to face her husband. "I had to leave the room, Ray, I couldn't stay there any longer. I saw the way Lord and Lady Planter looked at each other when Jacob was on about that letter. I knew it was a love letter from him, so much love and trust passed between them it broke my heart. I used to feel like that about you and I would like to feel like it again. I've been so lonely, but it wasn't until I saw that look that I realised what I have been missing all these years."

"What we've both been missing, Mary. I've suffered even more than you for what I did. It was too much drink and too little willpower. I never loved her, Mary. It has always been you. She seduced me when I was at my most vulnerable: when I was drunk. I can't even remember doing anything if I have to be honest. I woke up in her bed with a terrific hangover. I'm not trying to make an excuse but I suffer every time I look at you. I've wanted to take you in my arms and beg for forgiveness so many times, but you were so cold and aloof and I was so ashamed. I have to live with my guilt for the rest of my life. Even though I knew you didn't want me any more, just knowing you would be waiting for me when I got home from work was more than I deserved."

"We all make mistakes in life and mine is letting my hurt last for so long. I'm sorry too. Is it too late to try again?" she asked.

Ray strode across the room and pulled her into his arms and kissed her rapidly all over her face, then lingered on her lips until he heard her moan in respond to his touch.

Next morning, Mary woke to an empty bed. She hadn't had such a good night's sleep for a long time. She took a deep breath and let out a huge sigh of contentment. She rose to get out of bed and saw the envelope resting on the pillow next to her. It had her name on it.

Piling the pillows up behind her, she opened her letter. There wasn't much there to read but what was written spoke volumes:

WOW! THAT WAS SENSATIONAL! BETTER THAN I REMEMBER. I'LL BE BACK FOR MORE. XXXXXXXX.

Mary sprang out of bed with a grin on her face, threw on her clothes and went in search of her husband. She closed the bedroom door and took out her letter again, and was reading it when she bumped into her son coming out of his bedchamber. She hurriedly hid her letter in her dress pocket.

"What the devil are you hiding?" he asked.

"Nothing," she told him, linking her arm through his.

"You were you know, I saw you."

"Only a handkerchief," she told him.

Harriett, snuggled in her husband's arms, had listened while Nicky told her he intended to tell Sir David that he would drop her off at his home for a couple of days, while he came back to The Manor to sort things out with Jimmy. He'd come and get her from Sir David's and take her into Drunbury and see about getting her some new clothes, then they'd go to Berkwash and have a few days to themselves by the sea.

"That sounds very exciting; I've never been to the city before."

"Don't get too excited, it can be very smelly at times but I think you'll like it."

"You don't have to buy me any new clothes. There are two wardrobes full of your mother's clothes."

"That's as maybe but I want to show you off, Hetty. All my mother's clothes are old fashioned. I would have bought you some new clothes while we were in Berkwash, but time wasn't on our side and I don't think you would have accepted them if I had. Now you are well and truly my wife I can buy you anything I want, and I want to rig you out, so you don't have any say in the matter."

"Anything you say, my lord," replied Harriett, meekly, but Nicky wasn't fooled for a second.

The atmosphere in the breakfast room that morning was electric and Jacob said between mouthfuls of bacon, "What's the matter with everybody this morning, there's something going on?"

"I'm going to have to have words with you, my boy," said his father.

Jacob was about to fill his mouth again but stopped and said, "Have words with me, what about?"

"Diplomacy," stated his father.

"Diplomacy, what the devil are you talking about?"

"Language, Jacob," chastised his mother.

"Beg pardon, Lady Planter." He had the grace to blush.

"I can only apologize for my son, Lady Planter," Mr Brightman said.

"Please call me Harriett, and you don't have to apologize for Jacob to me, Mr Brightman, I like him," replied Harriett.

"I like him too, so no apology needed," added Nicky.

"Yes, me too," agreed Sir David.

"And I love him," smiled his mother.

Jacob looked from one to the other open mouthed, and then he looked down at his fork and said, "Wrenshaw, have you put something in this food?"

"Like what, sir?"

"How should I know? Some love potion or something," Jacob told him.

"No, sir, I have not," Wrenshaw replied.

"Then go and ask the cook. Something mighty fishy is going on here and it can't have anything to do with that letter. Now my mother's at it, she's had one of those pesky letters." Jacob cast a glance at his mother.

"Stay where you are, Wrenshaw," Mr Brightman told him, then he clipped his son playfully behind the ear and told him, "Eat your breakfast, boy, and don't talk with your mouthful."

"I ain't hungry," said Jacob, eyeing the assembled group.

"You had better eat your breakfast for you will not get anything else until we reach home. I need to get back to work immediately. I think he drank too much of that dirty river water and he has maggots in his head," complained Mr Brightman.

"I think the term is 'maggots in his top loft'," said Harriett.

They all turned and looked at Harriett who looked innocently back at them all.

"I suppose my son taught you that term?" Mr Brightman asked, looking at her over the top of his spectacles.

Harriett, instantly aware she had put her new friend at the wrong end of his father's pleasure, stammered, "I can't remember where I heard it, sir."

"In that case I'll let him off." Mr Brightman smiled.

Harriett and Nicky exchanged glances and Jacob, keeping a watchful eye out, didn't miss the glance. Something was definitely afoot and he was determined to find out what before he left.

"You look very fetching this morning, Mother," he said innocently.

"Well thank you, Jacob, I'm glad you noticed," she smiled sweetly at him.

Jacob looked around the table again and said, "In fact you all look like the cat that's got the cream, even you, Sir David."

Mr Brightman looked towards the ceiling and gave in.

"That's because I'm extremely happy, Jacob. I'm going to spend a few days with my daughter so we can get to know one another," Sir David told him.

Jacob looked at him in disbelief. "Your daughter? You don't have a daughter and even if you did it would make her a bastard. It's the food, it's got to be the food, don't eat any more," he told them all.

Harriett looked at Mrs Brightman and they could contain themselves no longer; they burst out laughing, adding to Jacob's confusion.

"There'll be gossip, of course, but if we show the world we don't care what they say about us then it will be a seven day wonder. Once there's no more pleasure for the tattlers to gain it will soon be forgotten, and someone else will do something and the tattlers will move onto them. I think it's a small price to pay for something as wonderful as having a daughter, especially such a very beautiful one at that. I think I can survive being talked about, after all it won't be the first time, and I've weathered the storm before with a less pleasant outcome," Sir David confided.

"I agree," said Mrs Brightman. "And if anyone dare disparage Harriett in my hearing, they will come off the worst."

"What! Are you saying Harriett here is Sir David's daughter?" asked the astonished Jacob.

"She is," confirmed the proud father.

"How long was I unconscious?" Jacob wanted to know.

"Not nineteen years," his father told him. "I think I had better take my son home, Nick, before he utterly ruins this new friendship," Mr Brightman said.

"As you wish but there is no need to run off, you may stay as long as you like. It's been a most entertaining couple of days. I've enjoyed your company and extend an open invitation to you all to drop by any time you're in the neighbourhood," Nicky told them.

"It's certainly been illuminating and I would like to return the invitation to all of you. In fact, Nicky, I insist that you bring Harriett to visit us whenever you're in Drunbury," Mrs Brightman said.

"Yes, and wait until I tell them all at the club I've met Lord Planter and he's invited me back to visit him, they'll all be green with envy," beamed Jacob.

Thankful his son was off the subject of drugged food and illegitimate children, Mr Brightman stood up, and after thanking Nick and Harriett they made their way out to the waiting carriage. Jacob sat up front with the driver while the three older guests settled themselves inside.

Once they were clear of The Manor gates Ray said to them, "I'm glad Jacob is sitting up top, that lad doesn't seem to be able to keep his mouth shut. I have something to tell you both. This will surprise you, Mary, as much as you, Sir David," Ray felt her stiffen. "No, my darling, it's nothing bad, I think you'll find it interesting. Some eight years ago I received a letter from a Freda Farnsworth asking me to keep an enclosed letter safe until I heard of her death. Then I was to get in touch with Sir David Murray and give him the letter. She said she had no money but she was sure, when Sir David read his letter he would reimburse me for my trouble. Freda left no forwarding address. She wrote that she had read in an old newspaper that Mary Daley had married Ray Brightman and he was a lawyer. Freda added that many years ago she was a friend of a Mary Daley and hoped she was the same Mary Daley she had known.

"I didn't tell you at the time because the letter was sent to me at my office and I was afraid you would ask me questions I couldn't answer. I thought it best to keep it from you. I put the letter in our safe at home. I didn't leave it in the office in case any of the other staff came across it, and I didn't want it to get buried under the mountain of paperwork because, no doubt, I would forget all about it. It didn't cross my mind again until Jacob came home and told us he was going to work for Sir David Murray and I must admit I had, on numerous occasions since making your acquaintance, Sir David, nearly asked you if you knew anything about Freda Farnsworth, but I didn't. I was given the letter as a lawyer and as such I had to keep it to myself.

"In light of what has happened, we now know that Freda Farnsworth really was your friend, Mary, and we also know she has passed away, so I am free to tell Sir David about the letter and pass it on. I think Mary, that your friend Freda, was watching out for Harriett even though she's no longer with us and the letter is telling Sir David that she is his daughter. That last bit is only a guess of course."

"How very interesting, yes, I think you're right. Isn't it strange how all this has come about?" said his wife.

On arriving back at the Brightman residence, Mr Brightman gave Sir David the letter he had received from Freda to read, while he went to his safe to get the letter addressed to Sir David. They had offered to leave him alone to read the letters but he insisted on them staying. He handed the first letter to Mary for her to read, while he took the letter opener offered by Ray and slit the second envelope open. He took out the folded sheets of paper, opened them and a locket fell onto the carpet.

He picked it up and said, "I gave this to Freda as a token of our love the last time I saw her," then began reading the second letter.

From: Freda West/Farnsworth

Hello David,

I'm sorry to say that if you're reading this letter I will no longer be upon this earth. I have asked Mr Brightman to hand you this letter when he hears of my death. This will come as a shock to you but, you and I have a daughter. She is beautiful. She is unaware of whom her real father is. I have kept it from her in case you have a wife and children of your own by now. What happened to me is of no consequence but be assured, I never stopped loving you. I have no wish to cause you any more pain than I have already but I had married a man who is not worthy of being Harriett's father.

If you could find it in your heart to help her once I'm gone it will help me rest in peace. We had a crofter's cottage in Reckly, near a village called Welldeck, about twenty-five miles from Drunbury. It wouldn't be hard for you to find, it's isolated but any of the locals will be able to point it out to you.

If you could help Harriett find a position away from Gary Farnsworth so she can earn a living, I could wish for nothing more.

I hope you've had a good life, my darling David. I wish we could have shared our life together and watched our daughter grow into the beautiful young lady she has become. But alas, it wasn't to be.

Goodbye my darling.

All my love, Freda.

P.S. Gary Farnsworth never knew I recorded Harriett's birth and named you as her father. I enclose her birth certificate. If you have no wish to meet our daughter then give the birth certificate to Mr Brightman and ask him to keep it in a safe place. As I have no money I took the liberty of telling Mr Brightman that you would reimburse him for his trouble.

Sir David, unable to speak, handed the letter to Ray to read who then passed it onto Mary.

After reading the letter, Mary said, "At least Freda will be looking down on us and she'll be happy with the outcome. I wish I'd tried to find her when she disappeared. I let her down badly so I know how you must feel, Sir David. I am so sorry."

"It doesn't do to dwell on what might have been. Even if Freda hadn't written this letter, you can tell Harriett is your daughter just by looking at her, if you were ever in any doubt about it," remarked Ray.

"No, even before I met Harriett, when Nick was telling me about her, I knew she was mine and Freda's child. We were so in love, we couldn't contain ourselves. I know we shouldn't have made love before we were married, we just couldn't help ourselves," confessed Sir David.

"If it makes you feel any better, I wasn't a virgin when Ray and I got married, we couldn't help ourselves either," Mary told him. "We were just luckier than you. We don't judge you, Sir David. I just wish you and Freda could have been together.

"I intend to carry out Freda's wish and look after her like a father should but that might be a bit difficult. Lord Planter is a force to be reckoned with. I shall be here for her if she ever needs me. I have a place in the country and I very rarely use it. I had intended to go and live there and breed sheep dogs but I think I am too long in the tooth for starting on a project like that. I'm putting my townhouse up for sale and shall sell all my furniture off. Would you be willing to act as my lawyer, Ray, in the sale of the house? I'd also like to make out a will. And, of course, add on whatever I owe you for keeping the letter safe," Sir David told him.

"I'll be delighted to act as your lawyer but I don't want any payment for delivering the letter. Harriett has repaid me more than she will ever know, it's the least I can do for her." Ray smiled across at his wife.

CHAPTER 13

Harriett made her way to the farm. Nicky had gone into town so she decided to go and see Jimmy. She hadn't seen him for a few weeks and she had a lot to tell him. Now Jimmy was happy and safe she didn't feel responsible for him any longer. He had made an impression on Nicky and was about to become his own boss, but didn't know it yet.

On her approach she could see him sitting on a chair outside his cottage having a puff, with not a care in the world. "Good morning, Jimmy."

Jimmy jumped up and came to meet her. "Harry, where have you been? Don't answer that, I've been kept abreast of all your comings and goings. If you don't watch out, Harry, Lord Planter will be throwing you out. It's about time you started acting like the lady you're supposed to be, not gallivanting all over the moor collecting negroes and floating bodies."

Harriett laughed and slipped her hand into his arm and they walked back to the cottage together. "That's where you're wrong, Jimmy. He's wonderful and he loves me. Who would have thought it?"

"Do you love him?" he asked bringing another chair out and placing it next to his.

"I do, he's just so amazing. You wouldn't believe the things he's done since I've met him."

"I can have a good guess at it."

Harriett laughed at his insinuation and carried on. "I've made some new friends, I've seen the sea and Captain Lally is going to show me round his ship when he gets back from Africa. And, you'll never guess what, I've found out who my real father is and I'm going to Drunbury and Nicky's going to rig me out in the latest fashion,"

"I'm so pleased for you, Harry. I've made some new friends too. I've some staggering news of my own, you'll never believe it."

"Tell me and I'll tell you whether I believe it or not."

"I want to get married."

"You're right, I don't believe it."

"The thing is," he continued, "I'll have to ask Lord Planter for permission and I'm not looking forward to that."

"Why do you have to ask Lord Planter? I would have thought you had to ask her father's permission, unless you are saying Nicky is her father."

"Of course I'm not you idiot. Her father has already given his permission, but because we both work for his lordship it's customary to ask his permission to get married."

"Who is she?"

"Her name is Sarah Brown. Her father works with Will Harrow and her mother works in the dairy and looks after the hens and ducks. Sarah is a chambermaid up at The Manor."

"I've met her. You sly dog, Jimmy Grayson."

"The trouble is I've got no prospects. How can I support a wife when my future looks so bleak? I've come to the end of these cottages, and Will tells me Lord Planter wants to see me today at four o'clock. You don't know what that's all about, do you, Harry?"

"Yes I do, but you'll have to wait until four o'clock to find out. You're such a worrier, Jimmy."

"We've always managed to come up with something haven't we, Harry? But this is different; being responsible for another person is a big step to take. What if children come along and I end up without a job. Who's going to look after them then?"

"If everybody thought like that then nobody would get married, and anyway, Sarah will be there to help and support you. She should take half the responsibility. You'll not be on your own and if she's willing to take a risk then so should you. It's got to be your own decision, Jimmy. If you don't want to marry her then you must tell her so. Don't marry her for the sake of getting married. Do you love her?"

"Yes, I love her."

"Then marry her."

"Everything is black and white to you, Harry, but then again, you weren't born with a limp."

"Oh, for heaven's sake, stop making your limp an excuse. You were glad when I came and told you to pack up and come here, weren't you?"

"That's different, there was only me to consider."

"Then it's about time you had someone else to consider instead of yourself. You're becoming morbid in your old age. You can always get married and stay celibate, then there won't be any children."

"What do you know about being celibate?"

"Nicky told me what it meant."

"I dread to think what the pair of you were talking about if you were discussing being celibate."

Harriett found this amusing and started laughing. "Some things are better kept secret."

"I'm pleased to hear it. Let's change the subject and tell me who your father is and how you found out."

The day passed pleasantly for Jimmy and Harriett. They sat out in the sunshine and ate bread and cheese at lunchtime, and while they ate Harriett told Jimmy of her adventures and how she found out who her father was.

That day was a very special one for Jimmy. There hadn't been many days in his life where he could just sit and talk with the sun shining down on him. He knew there wouldn't be many more days like this, spent with his best friend enjoying doing nothing but talking. Like it or not, they were beginning to grow apart.

Lord Planter, riding back from town, saw, as he neared his gates, a young boy trying to hold up a weary-looking woman. He dismounted and asked, "Is there anything I can do to help?"

The young boy looked round and said, "We're looking for work."

"How old are you?"

"I'm fourteen, nearly fifteen."

"And who is this lady?"

"She's my mother."

"Where's your father?"

"Never had one, with the devil for all I care."

"You'll have to excuse my son, sir, we are very tired and hungry. I was never married, an ex-employer took advantage of me, then turned me out when he found out I was pregnant. It has been so all his young life. As soon as it is found out that I am not married we are shown the door. Finding employment in my circumstances is nigh on impossible. I've tried to lie about it but someone always finds out. I find it better to tell the truth. I want you to know I'm not a loose woman, just tired and hungry. Now you know the whole of it," the woman said.

"What's your name?"

"Rita, Rita Stratton, and this is my son, Herman."

"Well, Rita and Herman Stratton, would you like to come and work for me?"

"Doing what?" asked the woman.

"I happen to have an apprentice carpenter's job going if Herman would like the apprenticeship, and I think Mrs Brown who runs the dairy may want someone to help her."

"An apprenticeship, for Herman, to learn a trade you mean?"

"I do, and the young man who will be training him is one of the best carpenters I have come across."

"You're not jesting us are you?" asked a suspicious Herman.

"Here, let me help you onto the back of my horse. It's a fair walk from here. You can sit side saddle and hold onto the pummel with one hand and the back of the saddle with the other, you look fit to drop."

Lord Planter took hold of the woman's thin waist and hoisted her up into the saddle.

The three of them set off for the farm with Lord Planter leading the horse at walking pace. Herman tried to find out more about the apprenticeship but Lord Planter told him to wait until they were settled in.

Harriett and Jimmy were still sitting talking when Lord Planter's little party came into view. Seeing them approaching Harriett jumped up and ran towards them saying, "Hello, who is this?"

Lord Planter put his free hand around his wife's waist and carried on walking until they reached Jimmy.

"Good afternoon, my lord."

"Good afternoon, Jimmy. This is Rita and Herman Stratton. Rita, this is my wife, Lady Planter, and this is Jimmy Grayson." They all shook hands and Lord Planter continued, "Have you finished that last empty cottage, Jimmy?"

"I have," replied Jimmy with a sinking heart.

"Good, let's show Rita and Herman to it. I don't suppose you have a bit of bread to spare for them do you, Jimmy? When you come up to The Manor later on I'll give you some food to bring back down," Lord Planter said.

"I have that." He went into his cottage and came back out carrying two tin plates with bread and cheese on each, and made them sit down in the chairs he and Harriett had just vacated. He went back inside and came out carrying two tin cups filled with milk.

"Where did you find them?" asked an interested Harriett.

"I nearly rode them down. They were standing at the gate looking in. Rita was ready to collapse, so here they are."

After they'd eaten Rita said, "Thank you, that was very welcome, it's the first food we've had for over twenty-four hours."

"The cottage is attached to this one, if you'd like to come this way, I'll show you round." Jimmy put out a hand to help Rita up and they all followed Jimmy into the empty cottage.

"Are you saying this cottage is for Herman and me to live in?" asked the stunned Rita.

"If you want it," replied Lord Planter.

"I don't have any money for rent but yes, I would love to live in it. We've been sleeping rough. We crept into hay barns at night when the farmer's lights went out but mostly we've slept in the open, weather permitting. It's beginning to get too cold on a night to be sleeping out of doors. I can't believe this is happening to us," Rita told them.

"There's no rent to pay, the rent is part of your wages. We'll leave you to have a look round. Meanwhile Herman can come with Jimmy up to The Manor and see if we can find a couple of old beds for you to sleep on. There are some up in the attic, you might as well have those instead of them rotting away. You can get a good night's sleep then. Come on, young man, you can start earning your money," Lord Planter told him.

"Yes, sir, you'll not be disappointed with me," Herman said full of confidence.

Lord Planter had mounted his horse and Jimmy helped Harriett mount behind him using his hands as a stirrup to throw her behind her husband, and she folded her arms around his waist and snuggled into his back.

Jimmy went across to the barn to get the handcart, and then, with Herman on his heels, they headed out.

Nicky turned and helped Harriett down from the back of the horse, then, jumping off himself, he handed the reins to the waiting stable hand. Taking her hand, he led her up three flights of stairs and to the ceiling hatch. Harriett climbed the wooden steps into the attic space followed by Lord Planter. The light from the skylight windows on either side of the apex roof gave off plenty of daylight, showing the extent of space that housed a vast amount of discarded furniture, clothes, toys and furnishings.

"Who are they, this Rita and Herman?" Harriett wanted to know.

"I've no idea. I found them at the gate looking towards The Manor. The woman was near collapse so I took them to the farm." He went on to tell her the story Rita had told him.

"Rita reminded me of my mother. She had that look of despair my mother sometimes had when she thought I wasn't looking, but I'd seen it, and it made me hate The Fat Man and wish him dead," Harriett told him.

"The Fat Man's gone now, Hetty, he'll hurt you no more. Don't let it make you bitter. At least we can try and make life a little easier for Rita and her son while they're here. It's also very opportune for us too. I had been thinking about getting someone to help Jimmy to set up this carpentry business and I think young Herman will do very nicely. What do you think?"

"I think you'll go far, Lord Planter," Harriett approved, "Does Jimmy know?"

"I didn't know myself until half an hour ago. Jimmy is coming to see me this afternoon. I was going to discuss business with him and find out what's required, but by the time we've got this stuff down to the farm it will be well past four o'clock. I think I'll ask him to come for seven instead. He can have dinner with us then we can thrash things out over dinner."

"That's a good idea, Nicky, then I can hear what's being discussed. Look at this, can Rita have it?" she asked pointing at a broken rocking chair.

"It's broken."

"Jimmy will mend it. I think she'd treasure it don't you?"

"I think she would, she may certainly have it. Look at all this stuff; it all needs sorting out and getting rid of. Anything you don't want can be given or thrown away. It must be a fire hazard."

"I would like to look through it first, Nicky, if that's all right. I shall enjoy hunting though all this stuff, I've never seen anything like it in my life."

"Hetty, my darling, it's all yours to do what you want with. Anything I have is yours. You can have whatever you want without asking permission. Ah! Here we are. I knew they were up here somewhere."

Harriett saw the wooden frames standing by the wall at the far side of the attic and went over to help Nicky carry them to the hatch. She slid them down the steps to Nicky who piled them up against the wall to wait for Jimmy to collect.

Nicky went down to meet Jimmy, and Harriett went on searching through the piles of stored items. She came across a big black box with a domed lid. Opening it she found lots of woollen blankets. Most had holes in them but Harriett knew from experience a blanket with holes is better than no blanket at all. They were piled up next to the rocking chair for transportation to the farm.

"Are there any mattresses to go with the beds?" Harriett called down when she heard voices from below.

"None that I can remember seeing, I think the mattresses were thrown out long ago."

"Then I shall put some of these old curtains with the blankets. I'm sure Rita will be able to sew them together and stuff them with straw. People with nothing are very good at make do and mend. There are some old clothes here as well, she might as well have some of these."

Jimmy and Herman began carrying the bed frames between them and Harriett came down and helped with the blankets while Nicky carried the rocking chair.

"Hetty had the notion you will be able to mend this," Lord Planter said to Jimmy, holding up the rocking chair.

"She seems to have a lot of good notions does Harry, and they all seem to involve me and work," he complained. "I've been a victim of these notions for the past ten years."

Nicky and Harriett burst out laughing and Harriett said, "I was put on this earth, Jimmy, to be a thorn in your side."

Jimmy chose to ignore the remark and said, "I'll see what I can do with the rocker if we can manage to get it to the farm. We'll have to make more than one trip anyway. The beds and blankets first though, then we'll come back for the rocker and other stuff."

"These old curtains too, give them to Rita. She should be able to make a couple of mattresses with them. Is there straw in the barn?" she asked.

"I'll sort something out for her. There are prodders and string in the barn, young Herman will be able to do that while I fix up the beds."

Carrying the bed frames through the hall towards the door, Nicky saw Herman glance at the bowl of fruit standing on a table beside the stairs. Picking up an apple, he threw it to Herman who caught it and put it down his shirt. "Aren't you going to eat it?" Lord Planter asked Herman.

"You bet I am, but I'm going to share it with my mother," replied the young man.

Lord Planter took another apple and threw that to him also. "Here, one each," he said.

"Thank you very much, sir, we'll enjoy these," replied a happy Herman.

Before Jimmy set off Nicky said to him, "Our meeting is going to have to be postponed until seven o'clock now, Jimmy. Come and dine with us, we might as well talk whilst we eat. If you see Will Harrow would you ask him to come up and see me as soon as he has a minute?"

"Very good, my lord," replied Jimmy.

Nicky and Harriett were still poking around in the attic when Wrenshaw shouted up, "Will Harrow's here to see you, my lord."

"Fetch him up, Wrenshaw."

"Will, thanks for coming. Have you seen your new tenant?" Lord Planter shouted down through the hatch.

"No, my lord, I had just got back from the cornfield when I met Jimmy and a young boy and Jimmy asked me to come up and see you."

"I came across this woman and her son looking for work. I've put them in the empty cottage next to Jimmy's. We're trying to sort some furniture out for them. Can you catch hold of this table top?" and he slid the top down the steps to Will's waiting hands. "I'm going to set the young man to learn a trade; I shall have Jimmy take care of him. Because the dairy is up and running again, I thought Mrs Brown would appreciate some help from Mrs Stratton, with the butter and cheese making. Could you sort it out and keep an eye on things? After all, we know nothing about them? Some of this old furniture is on its way down to the farm, Will, can you see to it that it's distributed equally and to the most needy?"

"Very good, my lord."

"Oh, and Will, Jimmy will be setting up a carpenter's business but if there is anything you want repairing, Jimmy's still your odd job man. Don't say anything to him about it because he doesn't know yet. You being the farm manager, I thought I'd better let you know about it first."

Will went back to the farm and Nicky, turning to Harriett said, "If there's nothing else for me to do up here, Hetty, I'll leave you to sort things out. I'm off to the stables to instruct Roy to get the coach ready for us in the morning. I'll leave you with your father for a few days. I shouldn't be more than three days before I'm back to collect you. I really enjoy doing these things with you, Hetty. I'd never have thought about coming up here and rummaging through this lot but it's been fun. You've brought so much into my life, Hetty. Come over here and give me a kiss before I go."

Hetty looked across at her husband. "If you want a kiss come and get one." She held his gaze with a wicked little smile on her lips. Two strides and he was taking her in his arms and giving her a long lingering kiss.

As he descended the wooden steps Harriett heard him shout, "I love you, Lady Planter."

"Glad to hear it, Lord Planter, don't you ever forget it." He smiled at her reply.

Jimmy arrived promptly at seven o'clock and was shown into the dining room. He had on his best clothes and his hair was neatly combed.

"I say, Jimmy, you look very smart," chimed Harriett.

"It's not every day I get invited to the big house for dinner. Will handed these down to me. He said he could no longer get into them. I thought I'd make an effort." He grinned.

Lord Planter waited until the first course was served then said, "Wrenshaw, would you mind leaving and coming back in about fifteen minutes."

"Very good, my lord."

"Jimmy, I have a proposition for you. I've seen the work you've done and I am very impressed. I would like you to do the same at The Manor. All the window frames for a start need renewing, some of the frames are nearly rotten through. I realise you can't be working on the windows when it's raining, so replacing the windows can be an ongoing thing when the circumstances permit. I have a few contacts in Drunbury that would be interested in your work; there seems to be a shortage of good carpenters. If I put the word out that I know an excellent carpenter, would you be interested in forming a company and going into business with me?"

"You're asking me if I would like my own business?" asked the astounded Jimmy.

"Partnership, Jimmy. I supply the work premises, tools and materials and you'll supply the goods. When work comes in we deduct expenses and what profit is left we share equally."

At this point Wrenshaw and the other servants came back into the dining room and served the main course, then left the room once again.

Jimmy having had time to think about what Lord Planter had said could only look helplessly from Nicky to Harriett. He could not find the right words to express himself.

"I take it that's a yes?" Harriett grinned.

"When I was given the cottage to live in I thought nothing could better that, but this, is too much to take in. Can I keep the cottage?" he wanted to know.

"You can if you want it but I think it would be better if you came to live in the cottage at the side of the barn up near the stables. I was thinking about turning the barn down at the farm into your workshop but Will wants it for the hay. There's a barn at the side of the stables that's not in use and it's bigger than the one down at the farm – you'll have more room to work. The cottage is a bit derelict at the moment. It is also bigger than the one you're in. I've seen what you can do to transform a rundown cottage into living accommodation. I'll leave you to get things sorted out. You'll only have to fall out of bed and you're at work. I don't think you'll have any trouble getting it into shape. After dinner we'll go and have a look and see what you think. You've already met young Herman. I've told him there's an apprentice carpenter job going as I thought you could do with some help. Can you take him under your wing and set him to work and teach him a trade?"

"I can that, my lord. He seems to be willing enough. He helped me set up the two beds, then I showed him how to make a couple of mattresses from the curtains that Harry had sent down and add some straw from the barn. I don't think he or his mother can believe what's happened to them, either. They've gone from starving and homeless to a roof over their heads. I know how they must be feeling, believe me."

"Good, that's settled then. Keep an eye on him, Jimmy. After all we don't know anything about either of them, so until they prove themselves it's best to be on the safe side," Nicky said. "Tomorrow I'm taking Hetty to stay with her father for a few days and I'm coming back to help get things sorted. We'll set up an account at the timber merchants, so you can get whatever you require without having to come running to me all the time. When we have things set in place I'm going back to collect Hetty and take her to Drunbury for a few days. I'll leave you in charge of things. I've also told Will, if there's anything he wants repairing, to see you. You're going to be kept pretty busy from now on."

"I wouldn't have it any other way, my lord. I'm looking forward to being able to have my own workshop, I can hardly wait."

"While we're in Drunbury I'll go and see Ray Brightman and ask him to make out a contract for us. I've taken a liking to him and I feel I can trust him. By the way, now we're going to be partners, call me Nicky."

Harriett looked at Jimmy with an expectant raise of the eyebrow. "No excuse now, Jimmy?" she told him.

Lord Planter looked from one to the other and asked, "Have I missed something?"

Jimmy replied, "I think your wife's referring to all the excuses I've given her for not doing things. But this is different, I want to do this, I really do."

"I was not referring to your new circumstances, Jimmy, and well you know it." Harriett looked him in the eye.

Jimmy had the grace to blush and stammer, "I was trying to find the right words, Nicky, to ask your permission to get married."

"You're getting married?" asked Nicky.

"I've been thinking about it, well more than that really, I was sort of pushed into it. Not that I don't want to marry Sarah. I do, more than anything, but my future looked so bleak. I've been backing off asking your permission to marry her, because taking on a wife when you don't have a penny to your name or even a job, is a scary thing. Now my future is looking so much better, I'd like to ask your permission to marry Sarah Brown?"

"You don't need my permission to get married, Jimmy. Congratulations, it will be the best thing you ever do. It's the best thing I've ever done," and he smiled across at Harriett.

Jimmy looked over at his little friend and said, "You'll never have a minute's peace and quiet you know, she's not a very restful person."

"I wouldn't have her any other way," Nicky told him. "I can't wait until there are little Harrietts running around."

"Heaven forbid," shuddered Jimmy and they all laughed.

CHAPTER 14

Nicky was driving the phaeton with its two big wheels at the back and two smaller wheels at the front. It was very well sprung and comfortable and Harriett moved closer to Nicky, tucked her little hand into the crook of his arm, interlocking her fingers, and laid her head on his arm.

"What's the matter, Hetty?"

"I'm going to miss you."

"I'll miss you too. It will only be for a couple of days, three at the most. I'll be back to collect you and then we can have some time to ourselves. Once Jimmy is sorted out, I know I can leave him to get on with it. Will has the farm well in hand so we'll have a bit of time to spend together, just the two of us, it will be fun."

"I know that will be fun, Nicky, but I don't know Sir David. I might not like him. When I found out The Fat Man wasn't my real father I was over the moon. Then, when my mother wouldn't tell me anything about my real father, I began to resent him. He'd deserted us, left us at the mercy of The Fat Man. Since I've met you I had even come to hate him for not trying to find my mother. I don't think I'll ever be able to forgive him, Nicky, for not trying to find her."

"Why since you've met me?"

"While I was growing up I didn't know any better. My mother told me about the balls and things but I'd never known what it was like, and although it sounded exciting I'd never missed it. Then, when I came to live with you and had a taste of how my mother had grown up, I compared it to what she was driven to. I can't help wondering why Sir David didn't come to find her. If he was so much in love with her he should have at least tried. If you went missing, Nicky, I'd move heaven and earth to find you."

"And I you, Hetty, it doesn't bear thinking about, losing you I mean. Sir David is very nice and I don't think for one minute he abandoned either you or your mother. Sir David became a recluse. He lived for his job and rumour has it he'd been scorned by the woman he loved and he never got over her. Word was, he never stopped loving her, that's why he never married. If Sir David had known how things stood with you and your mother I think he would have been there for you. Love is a funny thing, Hetty. It wasn't long before I started to fall in love with you but I held back from saying anything because I was afraid you'd repel me. We don't know what your grandfather said to Sir David to make him go away, and I don't think he's had a very happy life himself either. You also have to remember, Sir David didn't know your mother was pregnant with his child. If he had, maybe things would have turned out differently. At least give him a chance. It works both ways you know. Why didn't your mother try to contact Sir David and tell him of her situation before she married The Fat Man? They loved each other, I'm in no doubt about that, but I think pride got in the way of Sir David and shame stopped your mother from contacting him. How could she tell the man she loved that she'd been raped? It must have been very traumatic for her, Hetty, in fact, traumatic for both of them. If, at the end of these two or three days you no longer wish to have anything more to do with Sir David, then you have my full support, my darling. You have no need to see him again. I give you my word on that. I think you need to get to know him for your own sake as much as his."

Harriett gave a deep sigh and lifted her head to look up at him. "I love you, Nick Planter, and you're the wisest, kindest, cleverest man on earth; thank God for The Fat Man. I never thought I'd hear myself saying those words. If it hadn't been for him I would never have met you, and I can't bear to think about that."

"After some of the things that have been said about me, I never thought to hear that I am wise, kind and clever. I thank you for that. I love you too, Hetty, more than I could ever express in words. If you take as much love into the life of Sir David as you've brought into mine, then he will turn out to be a very happy man in his remaining years."

They rode on in silence for a while then Nicky continued, "Sir David has two properties. One a townhouse in Drunbury and the other is an estate about thirty miles to the east of us. That's where we're headed for and you're going to love the name of it, it's called 'The Squirrel's Dray'."

"You're right I do love its name. Have you been there before?"

"No, Sir David was a work colleague of my father. I only saw him a couple of times when he called at The Manor to see him, so apart from the rumours about him, I know as much about him as you. If his townhouse is anything to go by, I think you're in for a treat. I've heard he's a very wealthy man."

"We never had any money when we lived with The Fat Man but I had a happy childhood. I had my mother and that's all I needed. She protected me, loved me and taught me everything she knew. I know it's easy to say money doesn't matter, of course it does, but I don't think that's all you need to be happy. I think you have to be content with what you've got to be happy."

"At this moment in time, I'm more content than I've ever been, Hetty, but I'm glad I have money in the bank all the same, and I hope to keep it that way."

"I hope you do too, Nicky, and I hope Jimmy can make a go of the business and he becomes rich, then he'll have something else to moan about besides me and his limp. Wait until he's up all night counting his pennies," Harriett laughed.

Access to The Squirrel's Dray was gained via double wooden gates with a wooden arch above and the words 'The Squirrels' Dray' running from left to right. Sitting on top was a wooden carving of a squirrel holding an acorn with its fluffy tail curled up and over its back.

Nicky was about to jump down to open the gates but Harriett stopped him, sprung down and went to open the gates to let Nicky drive through. She closed them again and hopped back up beside him.

"You should have let me do that, Hetty."

"I'm not helpless, Nicky. What harm did I do by jumping down and opening the gates, we're a team aren't we? I think we work well together. I'm not one of those silly helpless girls that expect everything doing for them and I don't want to turn into one either. Is that what you want me to be?"

"I don't want you to change a hair on your head, Hetty, and yes, we are a good team. We do work well together, we're going to be all right you and I, Hetty."

"Yes, Nicky, we're going to be all right."

They drove up a long curving drive with trees at either side, which were beginning to lose their leaves but they still made a splendid scene in all their autumnal colours. The building itself was constructed of stone and two storeys high with small leaded windows and a red tiled roof. There was a covered porch and steps leading up to a huge wooden door. As they approached, a stable boy appeared from the other end of the building and took hold of the horse's head.

Sir David appeared at the door and welcomed them in. The entrance hall was spacious and well lit from above by a glass dome. A sweeping staircase came down from the first floor landing, ending on a black and red-chequered tiled floor. There was a large oak table to the rear, an elaborate, bronze, naked woman sitting on a prancing horse rested in the centre of it. Two straight-backed chairs were placed at either side of the entrance door. A large wooden coat rack with a mirror at either side of the coat hooks and two large vases stood on metal plates, one holding neatly folded umbrellas and the other a variety of walking sticks.

They followed him into a cosy dining room with leaded windows on either side of a set of French windows. Harriett noticed none of this, her attention was drawn to a nearly life-size portrait of her mother in her younger days.

Sir David followed Harriett's gaze and said, "I had that painted from a miniature your mother gave me. It's a good likeness, don't you think?"

Tears welled up in Harriett's eyes; she could only manage a nod in agreement.

"Tea is being taken up to your room and dinner will be served in about an hour. If you would like to go and freshen up, Jenkins will show you the way," Sir David said kindly.

Nicky went over to Harriett. Taking her hand, he led her out of the dining room and they followed Jenkins up the soft-carpeted staircase onto a wide landing, which went both to the left and to the right. Jenkins turned right and, when he reached the second door on the left, he opened it for them and said, "If there is anything you require please don't hesitate to ring."

When Jenkins had closed the door, Nicky took Harriett in his arms and held her tight and she sobbed into his coat.

"I'm sorry, Nicky," sobbed Harriett. "It was such a shock to see my mother standing there looking down at me with a satisfied smile on her lips. It was as if she knew I had found out who my father was and was pleased about it."

"I'm sure, if she had still been with us, Hetty, she would have been more than pleased about it. Don't you think Sir David must have loved her very much to have had the portrait painted and kept it all these years in pride of place in his dining room? Come on, wash your face and let's have a lie down for a while before dinner. Let me hold you until it's time to eat."

While they lay content in each other's arms Nicky said, "I have a confession to make. Do you want to hear it?"

"Is it a nice or nasty confession?"

"For me it was nice, very nice, but you will have to make up your own mind whether it's nice or not."

"In that case, confess."

"When we took Reco to Berkwash and we spent the night together in the same bed, you fell asleep. I couldn't get to sleep thinking about you lying there beside me. In the end I lifted up the bedclothes and devoured you with my eyes. When I dropped your dress to the ground and you stood there naked except for your bloomers, it took my breath away. I had to have more, so I took a sneaky peek under the bedclothes while you were sleeping just in case I never had the opportunity again. So for me it was nice, very, very nice. I take the image with me wherever I go. Are you angry with me?"

"No, I shall take the image of you lifting the bedclothes wherever I go. I rather like that image in my head. You should have woken me and made mad passionate love to me."

"Too tired I'm afraid, Hetty, but I went to sleep with a smile on my face," and he kissed the top of her head.

CHAPTER 15

After dinner Nicky set off for home leaving Harriett feeling uncomfortable and at a loss for something to say, while she stood on the porch with her father, watching Nicky disappear.

"Let's go back into the dining room, Harriett, so your mother can hear what we have to say to each other. I'm sure she'll be listening from up there. It's going to be difficult for both of us until we get to know each other. Let's go and have a talk." He held out his arm to her and she placed her hand on it and was led back inside.

"I'm sorry for not warning you about the portrait, but it is so much part of my life I didn't give much thought to how it might affect you. I'm not used to visitors. I've lived most of my adult life in seclusion and I'm ashamed to say, pining for your mother. She was all I ever wanted, Harriett, and she's left me with the greatest gift of all, a daughter. While we were travelling back from The Manor, Mr Brightman told me of a letter he'd received after he and Mary were married. The letter said Mary had been his wife's best friend in their younger years and she had read of their marriage in an old newspaper. It stated that he was a lawyer and your mother had sent him a letter asking him to keep a sealed enclosed letter, until he heard of her death. The instructions were to deliver the letter to me and I would compensate him for his trouble. Mr Brightman didn't tell his wife about the letter but he kept it and subsequently forgot all about it until the events of the last few days. Mr Brightman has given me the letter and I would like you to read it." He handed it over.

Harriett read the letter over twice then folded it up and placed it back in the envelope. "My mother told me she thought you would be married with children, and she didn't want to hurt you more than she already had by tracking you down and announcing my presence. She, like you, never loved anyone else, how very sad." She handed the letter back.

"One good thing has come out of it, Harriett, and that's you; we have a lot of catching up to do. We cannot alter the past but we can move on with the present. We had a dream your mother and I. We said, once we were married we would breed dogs, collie dogs to be precise, and sell them to farmers who reared sheep. It sounded so simple back then. I'm a bit too old now to start breeding dogs but I've heard of a farm a few miles away that has some puppies for sale. Would you like to have a ride out with me tomorrow and have a look at them? I've always liked dogs but I didn't think Drunbury was a good place to keep one. Now seems like a pretty good option, there's plenty of time to take it for walks and I thought I might try my hand at setting up a kennel service. You know, anyone who's in need of their dog looking after for a couple of weeks, I could do that. I would have to have some kennels built first though, to house them in, and set a kennel hand on to help out. That's if it takes off of course. If it doesn't, it doesn't matter; I have enough money to keep me in comfort for the rest of my life. If we set off early tomorrow morning, I would like to show you my townhouse on the edge of Drunbury first. I have no further need of it. I am going to sell it and all the contents, anything I won't need any more. I would like you to have a look around and see if there is anything you would like to keep, before anything is sold off.

"It will all come to you, Harriett. Everything I own will be yours one day. Nicky can have a look too to see if there's anything he wants but I think he has everything he needs. When the house is sold and I need to spend a few days in Drunbury I shall descend on his townhouse. Shall we go and have a quick look around the grounds? I would like to have your thoughts on where the kennels should be built, then, after dinner I'll show you round the house. We can have an early night and set off first thing in the morning. What do you say, Harriett?"

"I think I would like that very much, sir. I never had a pet whilst growing up. There was hardly enough money for food for us let alone a pet, so it was out of the question. I would love to go and see the puppies but as for any of your possessions, sir, I have more than enough at The Manor, but thank you anyway, it is most kind of you to think of me. Life has been going at a fast pace since I've been married. I seem to be being carried along on a cloud with a very strong wind behind me. I sometimes have difficulty in keeping up with all that is going on," she told him.

"We'll just follow the wind and see where it takes us, Hetty. I think the same wind is behind me, carrying me along too, and I don't mind it in the least. Life has become very interesting. I didn't realise how drab my life has been until now. Come on let's go into the fresh air and see where the best place will be to build the kennels." He stood up and went over to the door and held it open for her.

They spent a couple of pleasant hours wondering about the grounds and they decided the best place for the kennels would be behind the stables. Harriett told Sir David all about Jimmy and the business he and Lord Planter were trying to start up. Sir David said in that case, he would have a word with Nicky and give them the business of building the kennels. He would be interested in meeting this Jimmy who had befriended his daughter and had, to the best of his ability, tried to keep her out of mischief, but he doubted that he had had much success in that.

After dinner they set off on a tour of the house. It wasn't as big as The Manor, but Sir David had some very fine furniture to say nothing about the impressive oil paintings adorning nearly all the walls of the ground floor. The bedrooms were carpeted and fitted with large spacious wardrobes and there were heavy curtains hanging at the widows.

The room Harriett liked the most was the library. When you entered the room, the view through the French windows was breathtaking. It opened onto the well-kept lawn that rolled gently down to a lake. There were large floor to ceiling windows that flanked the French windows, giving the maximum light for reading. To the right and left again, from floor to ceiling were bookshelves full of multi-coloured books of all shapes and sizes. To either side of the internal door stood two tall cabinets, the top half of each being glazed showing beautiful glass drinking vessels and china tea services and plates. She bent and opened the bottom doors of the first cabinet to find it held bottles of spirits, bottle openers and coasters. The other had a drop-down shelf for reading or writing with shelves below holding paper and envelopes and anything one might need to write a letter. To either side of the cabinets a fireplace stood in each corner with a white marble mantelpiece above. An ornate mirror above each mantelpiece reached to the ceiling. A large leather-topped desk with a black leather chair stood a few feet away from the French windows. Two deep, red leather armchairs also faced the windows.

Harriett walked to the window and stood looking across the lawn towards the lake. "I think this is the nicest room I've ever been in," she said.

"I spend a lot of time in here, I'm glad you like it," her father said softly.

CHAPTER 16

The sun was shining when they set off next morning but the air was cold, and Harriett, dressed up warm, sat at her father's side in comfortable silence heading for Drunbury. They had decided to go and see Sir David's townhouse first and leave Harriett to look round, while Sir David went on to see Mr Brightman to set the sale of the house in progress before going to see the puppies.

They arrived at the townhouse about ten o'clock and were served a very welcome repast of tea and cakes. Sir David told her to decide whether there was anything she wanted. He was aware she had told him she wanted nothing, but he hoped she might change her mind and wish to keep something of his. He left her and went to get ready to go and see Mr Brightman to sort out the paperwork.

Harriett wandered slowly around looking in each room and opening doors, cupboards and drawers. She was on her way to find Sir David when she met him in the hallway, just as he was leaving.

"Harriett, have you had a good look around already?"

"Yes, sir, I have."

"Good, I won't be long; we can talk about things when I get back. Make yourself at home while I'm away. The sooner we get things sorted out the sooner I can concentrate on the kennels."

Sir David's butler appeared in the hallway. "Dinner will be ready in about an hour, sir," they were informed.

"Even better, I'll be off and back for dinner."

Left alone, Harriett went back into the library and she came across a set of diaries, going back to the day Sir David had met her mother. She took the first volume and began to read. The diaries told Sir David's life story and she decided she would ask him if she could have them.

After the soup had been served Sir David told the staff that he would ring when they were ready for the next course. They went out leaving Sir David and Harriett alone.

"Did you find anything you wanted to keep, Harriett?"

"Well, sir, I've been giving it much thought and to be honest there is nothing I need. I was brought up with nothing and Lord Planter has given me everything I could ever want. You have two beautiful homes, but so has Nicky. It's a man's world; will you be offended if I speak frankly, sir?"

"I would be offended if you didn't, Hetty."

"Well, sir, I would like to keep everything you were going to sell and store it for when our daughter is old enough, or fortunate enough, to have a home of her own. I know Nicky would provide for her, as I know he will provide for any children we have, but if we are lucky enough to have three children and two of them are boys, one will inherit The Manor the other The Squirrel's Dray, there will be nothing left for our daughter. If you left all your possessions from the townhouse to her at least she will have something of her own and not feel beholden to the boys, if she finds herself in an awkward position that is. None of us know what's in store for us but I would like to think, like my mother thought about me, that I have done the best I can for my children. I know we might not be lucky enough to have any children but it's no good selling everything off, then in twenty years' time, wishing we had put everything in storage. I think it would be a crying shame to sell all your possessions off to some stranger when I would hope your granddaughter would treasure your beautiful things. Unless of course you need the money, then you must certainly sell everything."

"Looking at it like that, Harriett, I would dearly like my things to go to my granddaughter and if there is no granddaughter then to my grandsons. I hope I'm lucky enough to live to see them born. I don't need the money, Hetty, and there are a couple of spare rooms up on the second landing at The Dray where we can store some of the things. We'll sort something out; at least we now know what we're about."

"I went into the library when you left and I came across some diaries you've written, I would dearly like those, sir, if you don't mind."

"My diaries, heavens, I had forgotten about those. You may have them with pleasure, I think you will find them heavy going."

"I don't think so, sir. I have read the first few pages and I think it will help me find out what sort of life you've had. I don't think I would find that heavy going. It will be very interesting."

"Then take them, they will only get burnt otherwise."

Sir David rang the bell and the empty soup dishes were removed and the meat course served, and soon after that they were on their way home via the farm to see the puppies. The weather had turned even colder so blankets were produced to cover their knees and a hot brick wrapped in a blanket was placed under their feet at the onset of their journey.

It was three o'clock in the afternoon when they finally pulled up at the farm and a jolly looking farmer came out to greet them, and took them to the barn where to Harriett's delight, six little black and white balls of fur came running over to greet them. Five of them were running around, pulling at the hem of Harriett's skirt but the fifth one sat at the back watching.

"What's wrong with that one?" asked Harriett pointing at the sad little bundle.

"It's the runt of the litter, I'll have to put it in a bucket of water if it doesn't buck up its ideas. No good as a working dog if it's too timid," the farmer replied.

Harriett looked up at Sir David who smiled and said, "There will be no need for that, I will take it off your hands for my daughter, that and one of the bitches. Which shall I have, Harriett?"

"That one with the white patch over its eye, it's cute."

"There you have it, sir, we will pay up and be on our way and try to get home before it's too dark to see."

Leaving the farm, with the two little puppies wrapped in a blanket cradled in Harriett's arms, Sir David set off at a steady trot but about two miles from home he had to slow his speed down to a steady walk. The light was fading fast and he didn't want one of his horses stepping into a hole and breaking a leg. It was turned six o'clock before the weary horses were led back to their stable for a well-earned rest.

While they were finishing off their evening meal, the sound of a horse and carriage pulling up outside and then heavy footsteps treading swiftly across the hall could be heard. Lord Planter entered the dining room still with his coat and riding hat on.

Harriett jumped up from the table and ran into his arms with a delighted, "Nicky, we weren't expecting you until tomorrow."

"I managed to get things sorted sooner than I expected. I decided to come this evening, and I hope you don't mind, Sir David."

"Don't mind in the least, Nicky, we've just about finished our meal but there's plenty left if you wish to partake."

"You don't have to ask me twice, sir, I'm famished," he said taking off his hat and coat and handing it to the butler.

"Have you been enjoying yourself, Hetty?" his lordship wanted to know.

"You bet I have. Guess what my father has bought me?"

"I've no idea," Nicky said pushing a fork full of food into his mouth.

"A puppy," declared his wife.

Nicky looked across the table at Sir David and said, "Please tell me it's not a French Poodle."

This brought a delighted laugh from Harriett who replied, "No, of course it's not, it's a tiny black and white collie dog."

"At least that's something," he replied, "I've never owned a dog. My father wouldn't allow me to have one and it's not something I ever thought about getting after he died."

After the covers were removed Harriett said, "Do you mind if I go into the library, Father, and have a look at your books while you two enjoy a puff?"

"You may go anywhere and do whatever you like, Hetty. We'll come and join you in a little while," replied her father.

So off Harriett went happily looking forward to searching the library shelves. She decided to leave going down to the kitchen to check on the puppies. They had been placed on a blanket in a large wooden chest near the kitchen fire to keep them warm. She'd take Nicky with her to see them in a little while.

Sir David looked across at Nicky and said, "I never liked your father you know. That day when you came to my house bearing the missing letter, I very nearly told the servant to send you on your way. If you were anything like your father I didn't want to know you, but I was too curious to find out why you should be calling on me at such an early hour so I decided to see you. I was all set to dislike you but when you walked into the breakfast room I could see you were nothing like your father, I was instantly at ease with you. I am utterly thankful I didn't send you away and I feel we will deal admirably together. So much so I have put my townhouse up for sale and when I need to go up to Drunbury on business I shall descend on you."

"I shall have a key made for you, sir."

"Thank you. I had everything sorted out in my mind, what I intended to do, but I hadn't taken Hetty into consideration and she has thrown my plans to the wind."

Lord Planter's face creased into a smile that reached his eyes. "Anything I can help you with?"

"I told her I was selling all the contents of my townhouse and took her there today to see if there was anything she wanted to keep, and blow me, she wants to keep everything. Two guesses why."

"I dread to think." He smiled.

"She wants to keep it all for your daughter."

"The devil she does. She intends to have a daughter does she? We haven't discussed that subject yet."

"Two sons and a daughter to be precise, one son is to get The Manor and the other son gets The Squirrel's Dray. Your daughter gets the contents of my townhouse. She said that she had all she needed at The Manor, she was more than content with what she had."

"Pretty neat planning at short notice don't you think?" Nicky grinned.

After a bout of amused laughter Sir David said, "Do you know, Nicky? I rather like the thought of my granddaughter getting my things and one of my grandsons living here at The Dray. It gives me a warm family feeling I never thought I'd have. I've told her that there are a couple of empty rooms up on the second floor here at The Dray where we can store some of the things but there won't be enough room for it all."

"There are plenty of spare rooms at The Manor; in fact the entire third floor is empty so if you want to store it there you're more than welcome. I noticed too, sir, that she's calling you Father, when did that happen?"

"At the farm where the puppies were for sale. There was a runt in the litter and I said I would buy it for her. I must say it came as a bit of a shock, not that I'm complaining, far from it. I didn't think she would ever forgive me for deserting her mother."

Nicky was silent for a few minutes then he said, "Two boys and a girl eh, that's something to work on."

"Well hurry up, I'd like to meet them all before I die," Sir David commented.

"I shall do my very best, sir," he replied. "Shall we go and see what mischief Harriett has been up to? Half an hour is a long time to leave her on her own."

Sir David knew Nicky was only jesting but he was more than willing to go in search of his daughter.

Next morning with their goodbyes said, Nicky and Harriett set off for Drunbury leaving the puppy (named Mini) with her father telling him they would call to collect her on their way home in two weeks' time.

The townhouse in Drunbury was all Harriett had expected. It was bigger than Sir David's and just as well furnished. He had a collection of paintings that Harriett found interesting and she would spend long periods of time in the coming years trying to find out about the artists who had painted them.

On the third day, Johnson, the butler at the townhouse, informed Harriett that she had a visitor.

Mrs Brightman was shown into the drawing room and Harriett ran over to her and gave her a welcome embrace which was warmly returned.

"Nicky went to see Ray this morning over some business or other and I happened to be there. He told me you were in town for the next few days. There is a ball on Thursday, Harriett, at Lady Cunningham's, and I would dearly love to take you as my guest. You will like Lady Cunningham, she's as big as a carthorse with a heart to match. I called on her before I came here and told her I was coming to see you and she insisted that I take you to her ball. Would you like to come?"

"To a ball, I would indeed, I've never attended one, but what would I wear? I've been to the dressmakers and I've been measured this way and that, then it was stand on this stool, then it was get down from the stool then back up on the stool.

I was never so bored in my life. I felt like throwing the stool out of the window then I couldn't stand on it any more. The dresses won't be ready by Thursday. On Friday afternoon I am to go back to try them on and bring them home. I only hope someone has broken the stool by then."

"Grab your bonnet and come over to my house, I'm sure there'll be something in my wardrobe we can alter and make fit for tomorrow evening," Mrs Brightman said.

Harriett didn't need much persuading. She went into the hall to collect her coat and bonnet and they walked arm in arm in the direction of the Brightmans' home.

Mrs Brightman took Harriett straight upstairs to her bedroom where they took off their coats and Mrs Brightman opened one of the wardrobe doors to reveal a range of evening dresses. An array of various coloured gowns in different materials met Harriett's eyes.

"What colour do you fancy, Hetty?" Mrs Brightman asked.

Harriett ran her eyes over the dresses and said, "I like that yellow one."

Mrs Brightman took it down and held it up for Harriett to see. "This one?"

"Yes, it's beautiful. Are you sure you don't mind lending it to me?" asked Harriett.

"I would give you the whole wardrobe if you wanted it, Hetty, I owe you so much. Anyway, you are more than welcome to this particular dress. The first time I tried it on to see what Ray thought of it, Jacob said I looked like a canary in it, so I took it off and I have never worn it since. You may change your mind if you like, now you know you'll look like a canary." Mrs Brightman laughed.

"I think it will go with my hair colour and yes please, I would very much like to try it on." Harriett smiled back.

The next hour was spent trying on some of the other dresses from Mrs Brightman's wardrobe but Harriett went back to the yellow one. The length was too long but the bodice fitted perfectly. The only concern Harriett had with the garment was the low-neckline; she thought it was far too revealing. When she looked down she could see her cleavage.

"You have a very nice figure, Hetty. This dress shows it off to perfection, I'm sure Lord Planter will appreciate it, and all the other men in the room if I'm any judge of men, which I can assure you I'm not." Mrs Brightman laughed. "I'm sure Nicky will have a nice necklace for you to wear, he'll be wanting to show you off to all the town."

"Does he know we've been invited to this ball?" she asked.

"Not as far as I know, I'll leave it up to you to tell him."

They took the dress downstairs and sat next to each other and nattered away while they hemmed up the dress. Harriett kept feeling the soft silk material and looking at the exquisite lace that covered the skirt. But the part of the dress she liked most was the delicate lace sleeves, that came to a point and ended in a loop that slipped over her middle finger. She had looked so elegant and ladylike and with her cleavage showing she felt very, very sexy.

"Just wait until Nicky sees you in this, his eyeballs will pop out," Mrs Brightman said.

Voices were heard in the hallway and the door opened to reveal a flushed Jacob. "Old Wilson told me you had a visitor and from his description it could only have been Hetty. How nice to see you, Hetty. Have you been in town long?" He came over and kissed her on the cheek, much to Harriett's delight.

"We arrived three days ago and we leave again on Monday," she told him.

"Why didn't you let us know you were in town?" he asked.

"Nicky went to see your father today. As for letting you know we were in town I haven't had a minute. Nicky has insisted he rigs me out in the height of fashion so I've done nothing but climb on and off a stool. Your mother came to see me and she has invited us to a ball at a Lady Cunningham's. I don't have anything to wear so your mother has very kindly given me one of her dresses. She said I could have it because you said she looked like a canary in it and she couldn't bring herself to wear it after that." Harriett laughed.

"If you think Hetty looks like a canary in it, I would appreciate it if you kept your thoughts to yourself, Jacob." His mother looked at him over the top of her spectacles.

"As if I would!" said the offended young man. "I say, Hetty, I'm going to the ball too. May I have a dance with you? All the other fellows will be green with envy."

"What, even if you're dancing with a canary?" she asked.

"When you're Lord Planter's wife you may wear whatever you want and get away with it, nobody would dare say such a thing, so that ain't a problem."

"In that case, Jacob, I would be honoured to have a dance with you," Harriett told him. "How have you been getting on, fallen in any more rivers lately?"

"Very funny, no I haven't, but I can tell you this, work isn't the same without Sir David so I have decided to call it a day and go and work for my father."

"Does your father know?"

"Of course he does, he's extremely pleased that I will be taking over the firm one day and so is my mother, aren't you, Mother?"

"If it makes you happy, Jacob, it makes me happy," replied his mother.

At dinner Harriett said to Nicky, "Guess who called to see me this morning?"

"I've no idea, Hetty. I didn't think anyone knew we were in town."

"Mary Brightman, she said she'd seen you at her husband's office and she came straight over here, after she'd been to see a Lady Cunningham."

"Oh yes, she was in his office when I called to see him about the contract for Jimmy. Did she stay long?"

"No, she came to invite us to a ball tomorrow night at Lady Cunningham's. I told her I had nothing to wear so we went over to her house and she has given me a beautiful evening dress to wear. It's very revealing though, Nicky. When I look down I can see my cleavage. After dinner I'd like you to see me in it and tell me what you think. If you don't approve of it, I won't go."

"What did Mary say about it?"

"She said when you see me in it your eyeballs will pop out."

"Did she indeed? In that case I can't wait to see it."

Nicky watched as Harriett slipped off her old dress and took the yellow silk creation and slipped it over her head, then turned round so Nicky could fasten the buttons up at the back. She held her hair up and bent her head forward.

They were facing a long mirror and Nicky watched her reflection in the mirror as the loose dress slowly pulled around her figure as he worked his way up the buttons. The end result staggered him. The neckline was just below the beginning of the swell of her breasts, revealing a deep cleavage. Her neck was white and her arms slender through the delicate lace sleeves. Her waist went in where it should go in and the skirt hung over her slender hips. The colour suited her perfectly.

Nicky took hold of her hand and brought it down by her side, letting her strawberry blonde hair fall over her shoulders. She raised her head and saw her reflection in the mirror with Nicky standing at her back. Their eyes met in the mirror and Harriett had no doubt as to what he thought.

"Do you like it?" she asked.

"I like it," he replied.

"Do you think it's too low at the front?"

"Hetty, my darling, I can't wait to show you off at the ball, I'll be the envy of every man in the room. The neckline is just perfect. Wait here," he told her and went over to the wall and pulled a portrait of an old soldier to one side and opened a safe.

He came back and stood behind her again and placed a gold necklace on her throat. The chain links fastened at the back with a single diamond clasp then came together at her throat, and the two gold strands were held together with another single diamond, bigger than the one at the clasp. The two gold link chains then became one and they fell further down her chest to be joined together at the bottom with another single diamond, bigger than the previous one, and rested fractionally above her cleavage.

"Perfect!" Nicky whispered.

"It's beautiful, Nicky. Are these real diamonds?" she asked.

"They are, but you outshine them, Hetty. Now I am going to carefully take off the necklace," which he did, then placed it back in the safe before coming back to stand behind her again.

"Now, I'm going to carefully undo these buttons so I don't pull one off, then I'm going to show you how you are going to make every man in that room feel when he sets eyes on you."

The gown carefully slipped to the ground and when Harriett stepped out of it Nicky picked it up and placed it gently across the back of a chair. He came back to her and turned her to face him.

"You know when Mary said that my eyeballs would pop out when I saw you in that dress, well it's not the only thing it made pop out." His eyes looked down at his crotch.

Harriett's eyes followed his and she saw the biggest bulge in his tight pantaloons. She looked up with an innocent look on her face and said, "Are you telling me that because I made that pop up you now want me to pop it out?"

"That's exactly what I'm saying, my darling, but let's start with doing that thing first shall we?" and his lips came down to meet hers.

She lay content, snuggled in his arms and he said to her, "I have been very remiss, Hetty. So much has been going on since we met there hasn't been much time for us. You need a wedding ring. There are lots of rings in the safe, Hetty, and I know you'll be the first to say it's a waste of money to go and buy a new one, but that's what I want to do. I want you to wear my ring Hetty, the one I intend to buy you tomorrow, so you can sport it at the ball tomorrow night, then all the men in that room will know you're spoken for."

"May I have an engagement ring too?"

"That is the first time you have asked me for anything. Of course you may have an engagement ring," he said and she felt his hand heading for her breast.

"What's this called, payment in advance?" she asked.

221

"No, this, my darling, is called pleasure, pure pleasure," he told her.

They stood outside the large jewellery store and Harriett looked in the window and through into the shop. There were ladies and gentlemen of fashion milling around, some standing, some sitting and others talking to the salesmen.

Looking up at Nicky she asked, "Isn't there anywhere else we could to go?"

"There's old Benson's at the other end of town but this is where you go if you want to be noticed," he told her.

"I don't need to be noticed, Nicky. Let's go and see old Benson, I'm always for the underdog."

Taking her hand, he started walking along the street. "I had noticed." He smiled down at her. "Old Benson will get the shock of his life when we walk in. If even one of the elite gets to know we've been to Benson's the word will be out and he'll be flooded. Let's see if we are trendsetters." His eyes sparkled. "It really is entertaining being married to you, Lady Planter."

"Let's hope I can keep it up," she replied.

"That's my job I think." He looked down at her and she was in no doubt of his innuendo.

"You are becoming very rude, Lord Planter," Harriett admonished but her eyes told the real story.

"All down to you again, Lady Planter," he said smugly.

And she laughed.

Mr Benson was a delight to behold; he sat behind a workbench working away. He hadn't even heard the doorbell peel. He was a slight man with rounded shoulders, long grey hair and a line-creased face. He was looking through a pair of gold-rimmed spectacles and his face was full of concentration.

Lord Planter gently tapped the old man on the shoulder and Mr Benson turned and looked up at him. "You should keep your door locked when you're working, Mr Benson, anyone can walk in, just like we did. It's not safe for you to leave your door unlocked with all these precious metals and stones lying about."

Mr Benson looked from one to the other and said, "Nobody comes here any more, lad, and at my age, what's to worry about? If someone knocks me on the head nobody is going to miss me."

"Oh, how sad, I'm sure there's someone that will miss you," Harriett said.

"Wife's gone long ago, so have our two children, daughter died in childbirth and I think my son was killed in the Peninsular. No, there's no one left," he told them.

"Not Donald Benson. Your son wasn't Donald Benson was he?" Lord Planter asked.

"He was indeed, did you know him?"

"If it's the same Donald Benson, he was the platoon sergeant of Lord Tandleson and I, when we were first sent to the Peninsula. He was a very brave man. In fact he saved Tandy's life. He was awarded a bravery medal but the army had no forwarding address, the address they had on file for him didn't exist. Because he saved Tandy's life, Tandy volunteered to take charge of his personal effects and try and track down his family. I know Tandy tried his best but with no listed address or correct date of birth there wasn't very much he could do about it.

"It's a time in our lives we don't talk about; we try to forget about it. We had been on manoeuvres and encountered opposition from the enemy. It was a bloody battle on both sides;

no one wins in war. We had defeated one enemy encounter and were on our way back to camp, tired, weary and hungry.

"There was a mountain pass we had to go through and the enemy came at us again, out of nowhere. There weren't many of them but they caught us by surprise. It was hand-to-hand combat and Lord Tandleson heard a cry of, "Behind you." He turned and saw a sword about to come down on his head but Sergeant Benson pushed Tandy aside and the blow caught Sergeant Benson on the side of his neck. The medics tried to save him but he had lost too much blood.

"It hit Tandy very hard and it was years after we left the army that he was able, at least, to put it aside. It's something you never forget. I think if Tandy could deliver his belongings and medal to his family it might go some way to make him feel less responsible for what happened. It wasn't his fault, it was the war, and I hope I never have to see such terrible things again."

Tears ran down the old man's face. "You knew my son?"

"We did indeed, sir, not only was he our sergeant he was our friend as well. I will tell Lord Tandleson about you and I am sure he will be calling on you at his earliest convenience, if that's all right with you."

"I never thought I would know what happened to him. He ran away to join up; he was only fifteen at the time. He must have lied about his age and given a false address to be able to get in. Someone we knew had a son who also served in the Peninsula. He was sent home, minus his right arm and he told me that was where Donald was, in the Peninsula. I never heard anything else about him so I presumed he was dead. Please, I would very much like to meet this Lord Tandleson and have my son's effects and medal."

"It shall be done, sir, I give you my word. The reason why we came here now seems very selfish under the circumstances."

"And why was that?" he asked.

"To buy my wife a wedding ring and an engagement ring," he answered.

The old man wiped his face with the back of his hand and stood up. "Life goes on, lad, I've found that out for myself. The young lady wants her wedding ring and she shall have it. Come and sit down and I'll bring you some rings to look at. How wonderful you came into my shop, everybody goes to that big shop with the fancy furniture and plush carpet. What made you choose my place?"

Lord Planter smiled and said, "In my wife's words, sir, 'I am all for the underdog'."

"The way I feel at this moment I'm far from being the underdog. You've given me a new lease of life, young man. Thank you for telling me about my son, at least I now know he died amongst friends."

Nicky dropped Harriett off at home, then continued on to his friend's house hoping to be told of his whereabouts. As luck would have it Lord Tandleson had arrived in town that morning and Nicky was shown into the library, to a genuine welcome from his friend who jumped up from behind his desk and gave him a quick embrace and slap on the back.

"Nick, my boy, you're the last person I expected to see. I called at The Manor two days ago and they told me you were on your honeymoon. Don't tell me the honeymoon's over already." He grinned.

Lord Planter smiled back and said, "No, Tandy, the honeymoon's fine."

There was something in the way Lord Planter replied that made Tandy's stomach churn. "What is it, Nicky, is Hetty all right?"

"Yes, Tandy, Hetty is fine but I do have some news."

"Good or bad?" asked his friend.

"Good I hope, but it might be a bit upsetting."

"How can good news be good if it's upsetting, for goodness sake? Make up your mind, Nicky my boy."

"I've come across Sergeant Benson's father."

"The devil you have," whispered Tandy in a small voice, his face turning white.

"He wants to meet you. I told him I would come and see you and that I was sure you would like to meet him."

"Does he know how his son died?"

"He does, I told him and he seemed relieved to know the truth at long last."

"What's he like?"

"Not much like the sergeant, he might have been in his younger days but I'd say he was about seventy now, if not older. He owns the jeweller's at the far end of Western Street. I took Harriett there to buy her a wedding ring. She didn't want to go to the big store and you know what Hetty is, she had him talking in no time and he told us his wife was dead, his daughter died in childbirth and the last he heard, his son was in the Peninsula."

"If I go and get Donald's things will you come with me?"

"Of course I will if you want me to."

"Don't think I can do it alone."

"You don't have to do it alone, Tandy. Go get the things and let's go and put the old boy's mind at rest."

When they entered the shop the old man was still sitting at his workbench but he wasn't doing much work. He sat staring out of the window and he was only brought out of his daydream when Nicky once again, touched his shoulder to get his attention.

He looked up and saw the two gentlemen he now knew to be his son's friends looking down at him. Tears started to roll down his face again. "You must be Lord Tandleson?"

"That's right, sir, I've brought you some things that belonged to your son, Donald." He held out the battered leather case.

Mr Benson took the case and held it to his chest. "I'm sorry, you must think me a foolish old man but I never thought I would find out what happened to my boy, and here I am with some of his things. I can only think of 'thank you' to say to you, but that sounds totally inadequate."

"I have kept them safe with the hope I could one day return them to you. I did try but I didn't have an address to go to. I can only say how sorry I am for the loss of your son and that too, sounds totally inadequate but I am. I am so sorry for what happened to your son," Tandy told him.

"Nay, lad, don't take on so. It's not your fault. He intended to go into the army no matter what I said to him. It was what he wanted. I tried my best to stop him but he ran away anyway to join up. He was only fifteen at the time, that's why he will have given a false date of birth and address."

"I think you may like what is in there, sir," Tandy said. "Beside his medal there are some letters addressed to 'Dad', no address on them, and a set of diaries. These I have read, trying to find something that would give me a clue to be able to return them to his family. They make very interesting reading about his time with the army. He also mentions someone called Sylvia, quite frequently."

"That would be his sister, they were very close. He never knew she had died,"

"Nicky tells me you have no family."

"No, they are all gone now."

"I would like to come and visit you, sir, if that would be all right, just to sit and chat about whatever you want. We could talk about your son if you like."

"I would like that very much. It's my seventy-fifth birthday on the twelfth of next month. If I last that long. Maybe you could come for a cup of tea then I won't feel quite so alone."

"I can do better than that, sir, I shall come and collect you at eight o'clock on the morning of the twelfth and I shall take you out for the day. Would you like that?"

"I would, it will give me something to look forward to. It's a long time since I ventured anywhere."

"Good, I shall look forward to it too. I think it's time we left you alone to read your letters and his diaries. It's been a pleasure at long last to meet the sergeant's father."

As Nicky and Tandy walked back home Nicky asked, "Are you all right, Tandy?"

"I feel as though a great burden has been lifted off my shoulders, Nicky. I haven't felt this good for a long time. I've a notion to try and get some of the lads together that served with us under Sergeant Benson, make a day of it for the old man on his birthday. Would you come if I did, Nicky?"

"I feel insulted you should even ask such a question, Tandy, you know very well I would come."

"Good, then I'll see what can be done."

CHAPTER 17

Harriett stood looking at her reflection in the long mirror. She didn't think she would ever have a nicer gown than this. It felt soft next to her skin. The necklace hung exactly where it should and the diamond on her wedding finger sparkled in the candlelight. Sally had fastened her hair up but left two ringlets falling over her left shoulder. Nicky had produced two diamond studded butterfly hairclips which completed the outfit.

"Blimey, I look good enough to eat," Harriett said to her reflection.

Nicky came into the bedroom his eyes full of pride at the vision in yellow. "You look perfect, just perfect, Hetty."

"I never thought I'd like dressing up as a fine lady but I've changed my mind. I feel very graceful."

"It's no good standing there admiring yourself in the mirror. The coach is waiting, let's go to the ball."

Nicky smiled at her and held out his arm. She placed her left hand on it showing off her newly acquired rings.

When they reached their destination Nicky said, "Watch where you place your feet, Hetty, there have been horses everywhere. We don't want you getting your pretty little shoes all messed up, do we?"

The entrance hall was fit to bursting with people milling around and Nicky placed his hand on Harriett's waist and guided her up the wide staircase, where he told the waiting butler their names.

"Lord and Lady Planter," he bellowed.

Harriett felt her face go bright red when she walked into the ballroom; every eye was turned in her direction. She was saved by Mary Brightman coming up to her and leading her off to meet their host.

Mary had been right. Harriett did like Lady Cunningham. She was so fat she could hardly move. She wore a bright scarlet evening gown that looked like a tent. She had an enormous bosom and no neck. Her cheeks merely carried on from her face onto her shoulders and chest hiding any sign of a neck. Her eyes were her saving grace: they were big and sky blue with long black lashes and they held a kind welcoming smile. Her hair was also black and it shone as she waddled between her guests. When Mary introduced them, Harriett's little hand was lost in Lady Cunningham's fat chubby handshake.

Nicky came up behind them and Lady Cunningham said, "I was told she was a pretty little thing, Nick, but she's more than pretty, she's beautiful."

"I can't argue with that, Lady Cunningham. Do you mind if I spirit her away for a while?" he asked.

"Not at all, I have others to greet. I'm glad you came, enjoy yourselves," and she waddled off.

"Thank you for rescuing me, Nicky. I have no idea what to say to anyone. It's stupid I know but I feel so tongue-tied. I am not used to this." She clung to his arm.

"There's nothing to be afraid of, Hetty, you'll soon get the hang of it. Wait here by the French windows where there's a bit of air coming in and I'll go and get us a drink. I won't be long."

Left alone Harriett pressed her back to the wall and tried to be invisible and in doing so she saw, behind the deep red velvet curtains, a young girl looking terrified.

She moved over to the curtain and whispered, "Are you all right?"

"No, I've just seen Roger Stanley and I don't want him to see me, please don't give me away," the young lady begged.

"Why would I give you away? What's wrong with Roger Stanley?" asked Harriett.

"He's hateful, rude, ignorant and big headed and he has fat wet lips. How can he think anyone would want to kiss them? He makes me shudder and, to top it all, he has this mother. She has the loudest mouth you've ever heard, it's cutting and vicious and she shows people up whenever she can. She and my mother want me to marry Roger, but I can't, I really can't."

"Why does your mother want you to marry a man with wet lips?" Hetty asked.

"Because he has a title, or he will have when his father dies. He'll be Lord Stanley but he'll still have wet fat lips," objected the young lady.

Harriett's mind raced, Lord Stanley – could this be the husband of the Lady Stanley, from whom she had bought Reco? She forgot her nervousness and started scanning the crowd. She was at a disadvantage because of her height but if she stood on tiptoe she could just about see over the shoulders of the gentlemen in front of her.

Whilst Harriett was on tiptoe trying to see if she could spot Lady Stanley, at the other end of the room Lady Stanley was in conversation with her host, Lady Cunningham.

"My dear, you'll never guess who has come to the ball, Lord and Lady Planter. I was so pleased when Mary Brightman asked me if I'd mind if she invited her friends, Lord and Lady Planter. You can imagine my surprise to find that Mary Brightman was a friend of Lady Planter. We have all been agog waiting to see what's Lady Planter is like and she turns up at my party. What a feather in my cap. I must say she is a very pretty little thing, and by the way Lord Planter was sticking by her side you can tell he is very much in love with her."

At that moment Lady Cunningham spotted Harriett's head poking over the shoulders of two gentlemen who were deep in conversation. "In fact, there she is, you can just see her face between Mr Jackson and Captain Cooper."

Lady Stanley looked in the direction Lady Cunningham had indicated and she saw a lovely fresh face full of concentration looking around the room. The temptation for Lady Stanley to make mischief was too great. She excused herself from Lady Cunningham and headed across the room.

Mary Brightman did not miss the two ladies looking across the room and she followed their eyes and saw they were looking straight at Harriett. She searched frantically for Ray but could not see him. Spotting Nicky talking to Lord Tandleson she ran over to him.

"Nicky, you have to go and rescue Hetty. Lady Stanley is making her way over to her and she'll eat Hetty alive. Lady Stanley likes nothing more than to cause embarrassment to others." Mary pulled at his sleeve.

"I can't protect Hetty twenty-four hours a day, Mary. She is going to have to learn to deal with people like Lady Stanley. I'm here if she needs me, but I can assure you, Mary, Hetty is more than capable of sticking up for herself against Lady Stanley. She'll be all right, trust me."

"Do you know Lady Stanley?" she asked.

"No, we've never met and if everything I've heard about her is true, I don't think I want to meet her," he replied.

"She's right, Nick my boy, Lady Stanley is a stinker. She'll show anyone up at the first chance she can. Best go and rescue Hetty," Tandy told him.

"I can assure you both Lady Stanley will come off the worst in a contest with Hetty. I am going to find this very entertaining," he smiled.

Mary gave Lord Tandleson a desperate look and Tandy said, "I think I'll just go over and stand by, just in case."

"Tandy, there is no need, I might not have met Lady Stanley but I do know Harriett and I am full of confidence that she will be able to hold her own. In fact, I am that confident I am willing to wager a bet, that Lady Stanley will come off the worst." Nicky smiled at his friend.

"You know something we don't?" asked his friend.

"I know something you don't, yes," confessed Nicky.

Three pairs of eyes watched Lady Stanley approach Harriett, two with horror and the other with interest.

"If you came forward to the front of the crowd you would be able to see much better. Why are you skulking at the back of the room? Can't you face society?" Lady Stanley appeared to Harriett's right-hand side.

"I had heard your name mentioned and I was trying to see you, Lady Stanley, to see if you were the same Lady Stanley I had met." Harriett held her eyes.

"You, know me, I don't think so," said Lady Stanley scornfully.

"I heard you were forcing your son onto a young lady that finds the situation distasteful. I was curious to see if there was more than one Lady Stanley. Now I see you it is confirmed, you are one and the same," replied Harriett.

"I have no need to force my son on anyone. He is courted all over town. There are females who would die to be married to him. You seem to be classing everybody as yourself. I believe your father forced Lord Planter into marrying you," her ladyship sneered.

"My, you are behind the times. I thought everyone knew that my father is Sir David Murray, and he had nothing to do with forcing Lord Planter into marrying me," Harriett told her.

"Sir David Murray's your father? Rubbish! Sir David is a friend of mine. I would have known if you were his daughter. Anyway, Sir David is not married."

"Then, if my father is a friend of yours, I will suggest to him that he chooses his friends more wisely in the future," countered Harriett.

"If Sir David is your father that makes you illegitimate, does it not?" Lady Stanley said with malice.

"Yes it does, there is no way that I can alter that fact, both Sir David and I are prepared for the gossip it will cause. Once it has been thrashed around town it will soon be forgotten. Everyone in this room is aware of the circumstances regarding Lord Planter and I and I can confirm it is true. After all it is no good trying to deny it. If the truth doesn't bother Lord Planter, Sir David or myself, I don't see why it should bother anyone else, do you?"

"I wouldn't want to see my son married to someone he can't respect."

"What about the other way round, Lady Stanley? Do you want to see your son married to someone who doesn't respect him, and finds his advances repulsive to her?"

"How dare you speak to me like that?" said the shocked lady.

"How dare you come into a crowded ballroom and start pulling Lord Planter and Sir David down? For myself I don't care, you may say anything you like about me, but I will not have you talking about those two gentlemen with so much venom."

"You have no idea who you are dealing with," spat Lady Stanley.

"And, I think, you have no idea who you are dealing with."

"And pray who are you to class yourself with me?"

"I am someone from your past and with one word I can stop your insulting verbal attack."

"You are someone from my past. I don't think so."

"Oh yes, we have met before, Lady Stanley. Fleetingly I know, but we have met," Harriett said with confidence.

By this time the whole room was hushed into silence, listening to their exchange of words.

"And what would this one word be?" Lady Stanley looked down her nose at Harriett.

Harriett leaned forward and whispered in her ear, "Reco."

Lady Stanley's face had a stunned look and she could find nothing to say in reply.

"I am not as cruel as you, Lady Stanley, your secret is safe with me, and, I might add, also with my husband. In future when you think it amusing to discredit someone you should look in the mirror first. And I would also advise you to leave your son alone and let him choose a wife for himself." Harriett looked the lady in the eye and Lady Stanley turned and walked away.

A little hand came from behind the curtains and Harriett turned to the young girl and said, "You can come out now, I don't think you'll be bothered any more by Lady Stanley or her son."

"Thank you so very much, now there's only my mother to face." She gave Harriett a wan smile and curtsey before she moved off.

Mary Brightman came across the room and took Harriett's hand. "Hetty are you all right? Lady Stanley is a nasty piece of work. What did you say to her to make her scurry off like that? I've never seen anything like it."

"Just something I know about her, Mary. Better you don't know and yes, I'm all right, a bit shaky that's all."

Nicky was by her side his arm round her waist. "Ace up the beautiful sleeve, Hetty?"

"Yes, Nicky, ace up my beautiful sleeve, but I seem to have dropped Sir David in it, he'll be the talk of the town. I didn't mean for it to come out, it just did."

"I know, we all heard. You have nothing to be sorry for, Hetty. After all, you said nothing but the truth. Everybody in town does know of our situation. Now it's out in the open it will be a seven-day wonder and someone else will do something and we will be out of the limelight once again. Once people know it doesn't bother us they'll move on and it will be forgotten in time. I was very proud of you, Hetty, you handled the situation very well. Who is the young girl Lady Stanley was forcing her son on?"

"I've no idea, she was cowering behind these curtains and I asked her what was wrong and she mentioned Lady Stanley. You can guess how my mind flew back to Reco. I wanted to see if it was the same Lady Stanley from whom I bought Reco. I never thought she was going to come after me like she did."

"I think you might have made a few friends here tonight, Hetty. There are quite a lot of people that have come under fire from Lady Stanley."

Jacob appeared in front of them. "I think this is our dance, Hetty, all the lads are watching. They didn't think I would dare come and ask you for a dance while Nicky's with you. They'll all be green with envy. I say, Hetty, you can dance can't you? I don't want to be left with egg on my face."

"You ungrateful puppy," Nicky laughed.

"Well, you're about to find out, Jacob, egg or no egg, here we go." Harriett held out her hand and placed it on his arm and he led her to the dance floor.

Harriett's first experience at a ball was one of mixed emotions. She hadn't like facing Lady Stanley although she had come out on top. She was pleased she helped the young lady behind the curtain and to top it all her dance card had been full. She had to turn down more than one eager buck, but in the end she was glad to sit next to Nicky in the coach going home.

"Did you have a good time tonight, my darling Hetty? I must say you made quite a sensation on the dance floor."

"It was all right at first, but I don't think I'm cut out for this sort of thing. I was becoming very bored with it by the end of the night. I'm glad to be going home."

"I was talking to Ken Bickford while you were dancing. He's a very good portrait artist and I have engaged him to do your portrait. I want you to wear that dress, Hetty, and have it hung in The Manor for all to see. I want you captured in oils forever, a perfect picture, just like your mother's."

Eleven o'clock next morning Harriett had a surprise visitor. Lady Stanley was shown into the drawing room.

"Lady Stanley! I didn't expect to see you," said Harriett.

"No, it took some working up to. I've come to ask you about Reco. Do you know where he is?"

"I do."

"I would like him back."

"That is impossible."

"I'll give you fifty pounds for him."

"I don't have him."

"Who does?"

"No one; he's on his way back to Africa to his wife and two children."

"Africa! You've sent him back to Africa?"

"That was what he wanted. He should never have been here in the first place and he most certainly should not have been locked up for the past three years."

"I bought him. He was mine to do with as I pleased."

"He was stolen goods. He was forcibly taken from his homeland and sold into slavery. You kept him against his will."

"I have needs. It's something I have no control over and Reco was the best at satisfying my needs. I want him back."

"I'm sorry, he is now well on his way home and there's nothing to be done about that."

"I'll take my leave of you then. I can't say it has been a pleasure making your acquaintance, Lady Planter, you have served me very ill." Lady Stanley stood up and started pulling on her gloves.

"Likewise, Lady Stanley. Meeting Reco was much more rewarding. Good day to you." Harriett gave a small curtsey but it was lost on Lady Stanley's back.

When Nicky joined her, he found her pacing the carpet. "I've seen that look before, my dear. Something's happened that has not pleased you?"

"I've just had a visit from Lady Stanley. Would you believe it, she had the cheek to say she wanted to buy Reco back. She said she had needs and he was the best one to satisfy them. Then she had the nerve to say I had served her ill. What about poor Reco? What of his needs?" She looked across the room at Lord Planter.

"Well, Hetty, I can understand what it's like having needs and not being able to satisfy them." He came across the room and took her in his arms.

"You can satisfy your needs anytime you like and well you know it, Nick Planter." She placed her hand on his cheek.

"In that case I shall take you up on it. After all, I am under orders from Sir David to provide him with grandchildren. Let's start where we usually start by doing that thing," and his lips found hers.

CHAPTER 18

Harriett was sitting on the carpet playing with her daughter, Freda, who was named after her grandmother. She was the apple of her grandfather's eye. Nicky was at the barn with the two boys who tormented Jimmy to death but he loved them like his own. The two boys ran off to play with Jimmy's three children while their father and Jimmy discussed business.

The past seven years had been kind to Harriett. She had borne three healthy children whom she loved very much. Nicky took the two boys everywhere and they idolized him.

A knock on the door brought Wrenshaw in bearing a letter. "This just came for you, Lady Planter." And he handed her the envelope.

"Thank you, Wrenshaw," she said taking it off him. She looked at the postmark and read 'Australia' and her heart skipped a beat. With shaking hands she took out the letter and read:

> *Lady Harriett Planter from Gary Farnsworth*
> *Rhodes & Rhodes Solicitors*
> *Written on Behalf of the above said Gary Farnsworth*

Hello Harriett,

I know you would find it distasteful if I were to call you Dear Harriett. I can assure you that you are very dear to me for all I have put you through. I want you to know I worshipped your mother. I can never atone for what I did, I can only ask you to try and forgive me.

We arrived in Australia penniless. The sailors on board ship took all our money. We thought we were good conmen, we weren't. It was a lesson well learnt.

Ronald took a job in a saloon, sweeping the floor for a pittance, but it kept us alive. We decided to move further inland. The weather was oppressive and at times the heat was unbearable. We headed up into the mountains and lived off the land. Ronald adapted better than I did.

I know you didn't like him but I think if you could have seen how he'd turned out, you might have changed your mind.

We came across an old man, near collapse, deep in a forest and Ronald took care of him. We became good friends. He was a gold prospector. He had a goldmine further up the mountain but he had never found any gold. He was too old and weary to stay there alone. He had been making his way down to civilization when we found him. He said if we stayed with him up at his mine he would leave it to us when he died. We had three hard years at that goldmine and never found anything.

When old Charlie died (that was his name Charlie Ringstone) we stayed on working the mine. At least we had a roof over our head. It was much like our little shack in Reckly; it was like home from home.

I was fast asleep when the noise and vibrations woke me. It took me a few seconds to come round and when I went outside I

241

found dust pouring out of the mine. Franticly I shouted for Ronald but there was no answer. I found him three hours later inside the mine. The roof had collapsed on top of him. The earth was shining with gold. He had found the gold seam that old Charlie had been searching for and never found. Too late for Ronald, you cannot imagine the loss I felt.

Not only had he been my son, he was my only friend and companion and the only thing I had left to remind me of your mother.

I worked the mine, amassing a vast amount of gold. It gave me something to do. But four years living on my own took a toll on me. I made some trips into town taking some gold with me each time and turning it into money. I was rich beyond belief; it meant nothing to me any more.

The doctor told me I had something wrong with my lungs and with luck I had six months left to live. I sold the mine and put the money in the bank, with the rest of it I set about putting my house in order. By the time you get this letter, Harriett, I will be dead and buried no doubt.

I have left everything to you, the money is being transferred to England in your name and the enclosed envelope has all the legal details that you will need to sign for the estate.

I know this can never make up for the injustice you suffered by my making you marry Lord Planter. (I must say I didn't like the man, too arrogant for words.) This money will help you to leave him and live your life out in comfort.

Take the enclosed letter to a solicitor, he will look after you.

I know you don't want to hear this but:

All my love, Gary Farnsworth.

With tears running down her face, Harriett jumped up and pulled the bell. Wrenshaw came in and seeing Lady Planter wiping tears away from her eyes, a look of concern came over his face.

"Wrenshaw, would you keep an eye on Freda? I have to go and find Lord Planter, I won't be long."

"Very good, my lady, it will be a pleasure." He looked down at the pink-cheeked, red-haired baby and smiled.

Freda on her part saw Wrenshaw standing over her and her face creased into a two-toothed smile with her arms and legs kicking out in excitement.

"It looks like Freda feels the same way," smiled Harriett. She was about to walk away when on impulse she stood on tiptoe and kissed Wrenshaw on the cheek, much to his amazement. "Thank you, Wrenshaw," she said and made for the door.

"What was that for, my lady?"

"For all your hard work, Wrenshaw. I just had a vision of my life before I came to The Manor and thank my lucky stars." She turned and set off running down to the barn with the letter clutched in her hand.

Wrenshaw looked down at the smiling baby and, bending down, he scooped her up and said to her, "Shall we go and see the ducks?"

He walked out of the room with her and found her perambulator, picked up her bonnet and went back into the parlour where he sat down on the sofa and attempted to tie the bonnet on her shock of red hair. He found it more difficult than he expected. Freda wouldn't keep still, she wriggled and turned and tried to climb up Wrenshaw's waistcoat, until in the end, he went back out into the hall, sat her in her perambulator and fastened her reins. Taking the bonnet he placed it on her little head and now having two free hands he was able to tie a bow under her chin. He stood back and surveyed his handiwork with satisfaction.

Not used to being in charge of a baby, he didn't want to leave the perambulator unattended, so he manoeuvred it and headed back into the parlour where he rang the bell and waited for the second butler to appear.

A tap on the door and James entered. His mouth dropped open when he observed the straight-laced Wrenshaw standing holding the perambulator, and he was even more shocked when Wrenshaw said, "Nip down to the kitchen, would you, James, and bring me back a chunk of bread."

"A chunk of bread, Mr Wrenshaw?" questioned the young man.

"Yes, James, a chunk of bread."

"Very good, Mr Wrenshaw," replied the junior.

"Oh and, James, I thought I had taught you better than to question a request for your services. If you want to take over from me, in future, if you are asked to do something, you had better do it without question, or shocked expression on your face, is that clear?"

"Take over from you, Mr Wrenshaw, whatever do you mean?"

"I mean, James, I am going to retire and as you are second-in-command I expect you to behave in the correct manner, or you might find yourself replaced with a more respectful servant. Do I make myself clear?"

"Perfectly, Mr Wrenshaw, I will bring you your bread." The young man bowed out.

On his return James handed Mr Wrenshaw his bread and said, "If his lordship should ask of your whereabouts, what shall I tell him?"

"Tell him we've gone to feed the ducks." He smiled and pushed on past his shocked underling.

Harriett opened the barn door and, seeing Nicky standing talking to Jimmy, ran straight into his arms and burst into tears.

"What on earths wrong?" he asked. "Freda?"

"Freda's all right I left her with Wrenshaw," sobbed Harriett, and handed him the letter which he read while she composed herself.

Jimmy looked on with a frown and when Nicky had read the letter he handed it to Jimmy to read. He knew Harriett wouldn't mind. If he hadn't handed him the letter she would have done so.

Having read the letter Jimmy snorted in disgust and said, "Good God, Harry, surely you're not crying over that old scoundrel. Good riddance to bad rubbish I say."

This brought Harriett back to earth and she said, "It was a bit of a shock. It was the last thing I expected, to hear from him, and what about Ronald being buried under a ton of gold?"

"I'm sorry for that, Harry, but it still doesn't alter things. The Fat Man was still manipulating Ronald by the sounds of things, making him do all the work and living off him. He was even in bed when the roof collapsed. Don't waste your time feeling sorry for either of them. They touched a lot of people's lives and not for the better. Look what he did to your mother and grandfather to say nothing about Sir David, a nicer man you couldn't wish to meet. If it hadn't been for The Fat Man he might have had a happier life. Just because he's dead it doesn't make what he did any better. He's still trying to manipulate you, Harry, even from the other side of the world. He has made you uncertain and unsure, don't let him do it to you, Harry, take the money and help Nick out. Bringing up three children isn't cheap. Use him, Harry, for once in your life. Take the money and enjoy it, I know I would," Jimmy told her.

"What do you think, Nicky?"

"I must admit I agree with Jimmy, Hetty. It wouldn't surprise me if The Fat Man and his Toad didn't swindle the old gold prospector out of the mine. Just because he's sent you a gushing letter it doesn't make him any the better. I think Jimmy's right, take the money and let's help make a few people's lives better with it. We can put some of the money into the business and employ more people. The old cottages need knocking down and some new accommodation building with more rooms for the families. I've also even been thinking of building Jimmy a new home, one that befits his standing and letting old Wrenshaw retire to Jimmy's old cottage. I noticed poor old Wrenshaw struggling up the stairs the other day. I think he's worked long enough. It's time for him to take things easier now. There are all kinds of things we could use the money for, Hetty, if you don't want it. Take the money and be done with him, he can hurt you no more. The Fat Man is dead, time to celebrate." Nicky looked down at her.

"Let's have a party then."

"Good idea," agreed Nicky and Jimmy in unison.

On entering The Manor, Lord Planter was surprised to see James standing in the hallway. "Where's Wrenshaw?" he asked.

"They've gone to feed the ducks, my lord," James informed them.

"They, who are they? Gone to feed the ducks you say. What the devil are you talking about, James?" he wanted to know.

"The bell rang, my lord, and Mr Wrenshaw was nowhere to be seen so I answered it. I found Mr Wrenshaw in the parlour with Miss Freda in her perambulator, and he asked me to go and see cook and get him a chunk of bread, my lord." James waited for a response.

"What did he say exactly?" Lord Planter wanted to know.

"When he asked me to go get him some bread, I was momentarily shocked and I said, 'A chunk of bread, Mr Wrenshaw?' and he said, 'I thought I had trained you better than that James, to question your superiors. You're going to have to do better than that now you are in charge.' I was stunned, my lord. I asked him what he meant and he said, 'I have decided to retire, James, I'm leaving you in charge, now go and get me the bread and be quick about it.'

"I ran back to the kitchen and got his bread and brought it back to him, and he took it saying, 'Thank you, James,' and started heading for the door pushing the pram. I asked him what I should tell you if you enquired about him and that's what he told me to tell you. He said, 'Tell them we've gone to feed the ducks,' and that's all I can tell you, my lord."

"In that case, James, it looks like you've been promoted. We'd better see about giving you a rise and sorting Wrenshaw out some accommodation, then you can move into his quarters as befits your status," Lord Planter told him and he led Harriett into the parlour.

"Heavens, Hetty, I know I was just saying it's about time Wrenshaw retired and I'm pleased he has taken the leap himself. I would have hated having to tell him it's about time he retired. But that's not what scares me. It's Freda, Hetty, it frightens the life out of me," he told her.

"Freda! She's only six months old, what on earth can scare you about that for heaven's sake?" asked his wife.

"That's exactly the point, Hetty, she's only six months old and already she's got your father wrapped round her little finger and now Wrenshaw's doting on her. What's it going to be like when she's eighteen, we'll have all the young bucks in the district dallying after her?"

"She will have lived with her father for eighteen or so years, any young buck trying to lead her astray will have a lot to live up to. She will compare them to you. She'll be all right, there's nothing to worry about. Anyway I'm sure you'll do the right thing when the time comes." Harriett laughed.

"Too true I will, I'll knock their blocks off, that's what I'll do," said Lord Planter with feeling.

"Yes, dear, I knew you'd know what to do." His wife smiled sweetly at him. "It would seem to me that it's not only my father and Wrenshaw that are wrapped round her little finger."

Lord Planter looked over at his wife and said, "Come over here and give me a kiss. She complied only to be quickly released when a knock came to the door and Wrenshaw appeared pushing the perambulator.

"Wrenshaw, you're back. Did Freda like the ducks?" Harriett smiled at him.

"She liked the ducks right enough but I don't think she quite got the hang of the bread. Every time I broke off a piece of bread for her to throw for the ducks, she tried to eat it," he told them.

This brought a delighted laugh from Harriett and she went over to take her daughter out of the pram.

"I shouldn't do that, my lady, she's a bit wet in the nether regions and a bit more besides by the smell of things," Wrenshaw said.

"Poor, Freda, Wrenshaw has relegated you to a life in the pram just because you have filled your nappy. Naughty, naughty Wrenshaw," she told her daughter as she unfastened the reins and lifted her out and gave her a big hug. "If you intend to take her out in future, Wrenshaw, you'll have to get into the habit of taking spare nappies with you and a bottle of milk too. Babies soon get hungry you know."

"Very well, my lady, I'll bear that in mind," he told her. "May I have a word, my lord?" he asked Nicky.

"I'll just take the smelly Freda up to the nursery then shall I?" Harriett asked.

"You may stay if you wish, my lady, you will have to hear this too," Wrenshaw told her.

"No, I need to see to this little lady. I'll leave you two to sort out whatever needs sorting out. Nicky will tell me later." As Harriett was closing the door behind her they heard her say to Freda, "Have you been trying to eat the duck duck's bread?"

"Sit down, Wrenshaw." Lord Planter pointed to a chair.

"No thank you, my lord, I'll stand," replied Wrenshaw.

"For heaven's sake sit down, man, take the weight off your feet, we have things to discuss I believe."

"Very well, my lord," said Wrenshaw as he gratefully eased his old bones into an easy chair.

"Here, have a brandy. I think you'll need it after pushing that pram up from the farm." Lord Planter handed him a glass.

"Much obliged I'm sure." Wrenshaw took the offered glass.

"Now I believe you have decided to retire, is that right?"

"It is indeed, my lord. I think you'll find James a worthy replacement, he's a good lad."

"You'll be sadly missed, Wrenshaw. You've been a good, loyal servant. There's a spare cottage down on the farm that Jimmy used to occupy if that's what you want. A little place of your own and of course a small pension will go with it. You will be welcome up at The Manor to see your old friends and work colleagues any time you wish and we'll be pleased to see you too."

"I've a mind to have the cottage, my lord, and I look forward to having time to take the boys fishing. They keep asking me to take them but of course, while I've been working, I couldn't. The thought of having nothing to do but laze about on the riverbank with the boys has been preying on my mind for the past few months. When Lady Planter asked me to look after Miss Freda for an hour, I decided to take a chance on it and see if I liked having no work to do, and you know what, I loved it. I so enjoyed taking her down to the duck pond and seeing her little face light up when she saw the hens and ducks and geese. I only brought her back when she started to smell worse than the farmyard. I don't think I could do that, my lord, you know, change the nappies, don't think I have the stomach for it," he admitted.

"You and me both, Wrenshaw, you and me both." And they lifted their glasses up and drank a silent thanks that it was not their lot.

CHAPTER 19

Life down on the farm had taken a turn of the unexpected for more than one of the inhabitants. Mr Harrow, fifty years old and a confirmed bachelor, had taken to visiting Mrs Stratton every Sunday for his dinner. Then every Wednesday evening for supper, and on the nights that he didn't go to dine, he made sure he was around to have a few words with her if he saw her outside her cottage. He found he was disappointed if days went by without as much as a good morning being spoken between them.

He knew about her having a child out of wedlock and he also knew what she had done to keep herself and her son alive. He had also had a hard time supporting himself earlier on in his life and he had nothing but admiration for her. Her son, young Herman, was a pleasant hardworking young man being only fourteen years old when they had first come to The Manor and now, seven years on he was twenty-one and had a girl of his own.

Mr Harrow pulled at his tight shirt collar then wiped his hands down his trousers. He had made his decision. He was going to ask Mrs Stratton to marry him. It was the biggest thing he had ever done in his life. He was used to his own company but since meeting Mrs Stratton he had become more and more aware of how lonely he was. Getting to fifty and thinking about getting married brought him out in a cold sweat.

A knock to the door brought him to his senses and he opened it to find Herman standing there. "Mum sent me to see if you were all right. Dinner's ready, it's been ready these past ten minutes."

"Sorry, lad, I've been having trouble with this neckerchief, not used to wearing them."

"There is no need to get dressed up, Mr Harrow," Herman said. "There's only Mum, Jane and I and you've met Jane before."

"Well, lad, it's like this, I've seen how you and Jane are and I've been having thoughts about moving your mother over here and leaving your cottage for you and Jane, if that's what you want." Will Harrow pulled again at his collar.

"Mum is a very proud woman, Mr Harrow; I think she would be very insulted if you asked her to move in with you. Just because she had me out of wedlock doesn't mean she's a loose woman and anyway, I wouldn't let her move out just to let me have the cottage," said an angry Herman.

"Nay, lad, you've got it all wrong. I want to marry the lass, never met anyone before that I could live comfortably with until I met your mother. If she'll have me that is, I'm no prize catch. I've been putting off asking her, and putting off asking her until the years have rolled round, it's now or never. I'm as nervous as a teenager. If she says yes, that will make me your stepfather, any objections to that?" Will asked him.

"None whatsoever, but it will have to be my mother's decision. If and when Jane and I get married she can stay with us if she wants to. Jane and my mother get on very well," replied Herman.

"At least that's one obstacle overcome." Will sighed. "Better get going then or I'll be in trouble before I start."

After dinner Herman asked Jane if she'd like to go for a walk and Will found himself alone with Rita. His collar begin to choke him again, he tugged nervously at it.

"Is there something wrong, Will?" asked Rita. "You look uncomfortable."

"Not used to wearing a collar," he told her.

"Then unfasten it if it's uncomfortable," she said.

"Not until you've heard what I have so say to you." He blushed.

"Better get on with it before you choke to death then, I'd miss your company." She smiled at him.

"Would you, would you miss me if I wasn't here?" he asked eagerly.

"You know I would, we've been good friends since I arrived here. We've never had a fallout have we?"

"No, we haven't. I wondered if you would like to move in with me?" he blurted out.

Silence fell in the cottage and Will held his breath and waited for her to reply.

"As what?" she asked.

"My wife of course, what else could I mean? I've been a bachelor for far too long and I miss you when I close my door. I thought I liked being alone but that's all changed since I met you. I know I'm not much of a catch, Rita, but I have come to love you and I miss you when we're apart. I had a word with young Herman when he came to see where I was and asked him if he minded me being his stepfather and he said no, so you can't make Herman an excuse." He stood up and looked across at her.

"As if I need an excuse to say I'll marry you. Of course I'll marry you, Will Harrow. Lord, I thought you'd never ask. Come here," she ordered, and when he came she reached up and unfastened his collar.